He was gone, and she was pregnant. How was she going to survive?

When Jamie didn't show up after four days, Abby called his office and was told that they had not heard from him. She was told not to worry and that they would check with the office in Leadville and see what information they could gather.

When the Leadville office reported that Jamie had not shown up, mild panic ensued at the Denver office of the National Park Service. An all-out search was ordered, and Park Service employees from all over the state headed for the White River National Forest area. Eventually, the truck was found at the crash site, but there was no sign of Jamie Cain anywhere, no blood no evidence of an attack by a bear or some other animal, and no footsteps leading away from the crash site. It was a complete mystery.

Two rangers were sent to Jamie's parents' house to inform them. Jamie's mother called Abby and told her. Mrs. Cain offered to come and get her, but Abby said she would drive to the Cains' house. The Cains were frantic when Abby arrived, and Abby wasn't much better.

"They have to find him, Mrs. Cain. They have to. I don't want to live without Jamie."

"Let's not jump to conclusions, Abby. They have a lot of people out looking for him. He was not killed in the accident, and there were no signs of trauma at the scene. Let's just hope and pray they find him."

"We were going to get married in four months. Oh, God, what am I going to do?" She broke down completely.

Their lives and love interrupted by tragic circumstances beyond their control, Jamie Cain and Abby Prentiss are forced to go their separate ways. Believing him to be dead, she begins a new life she never really wanted but pursues out of necessity and self-preservation. Rescued from death, he searches for her for fourteen years and, at the point of giving up hope of ever finding her, a miraculous encounter, with the daughter he didn't know he had, brings her back into his life. But to what end? He has been searching for her half his life, while she has moved on. Is there any hope for their love at this late stage?

KUDOS for *Dreams Once Dreamed*

In *Dreams Once Dreamed* by Jack Sprouse, Jamie Cain and Abby Prentiss are high school sweethearts who plan to marry as soon as they can. But a few months before the wedding, Jamie is in an auto accident and disappears. Fearing he is dead, Abby leaves town because she has discovered she is pregnant and can't face the memories in Jamie's hometown. But Jamie isn't dead. He hit his head when his truck went over a cliff and has amnesia. Once his memory returns, he starts searching for Abby, but she left no forwarding address, and Jamie's search stretches out to a long fourteen years. Imagine his surprise when he runs into his teenage daughter quite by chance. A touching and heartwarming story of love too strong to forget, it will make you smile all the way through. A really good read. ~ *Taylor Jones, The Review Team of Taylor Jones & Regan Murphy*

Dreams Once Dreamed is the story of two people who were meant to be together but were torn apart by circumstances beyond their control. When Jamie Cain meets Abby Prentiss in high school, it is love at first sight. They graduate and plan to marry, but fate intervenes. Four months before their wedding, Jamie, who is working for the state park service, rolls his truck and hits his head on a rock when he is thrown from the vehicle, giving himself a concussion and temporary amnesia. He is rescued by an old hermit widow woman, who takes him to her home in the forest and nurses him back to health. He stay with her for six months, while the park rangers search for him and his family and Abby think he's dead. Shortly after he disappears, Abby discovers she's pregnant. She and her mother leave town and go to live with Abby's aunt some two hundred miles away. When Jamie regains his memory, he immediately starts searching for Abby, but she is long gone. Fourteen long years later, on the point of giving up, he has a chance encounter with a young woman in a convenience store who claims to be his daughter. *Dreams Once Dreamed* is the story of love, devotion, and courage in the face of challenging circumstances. It will break your heart and warm it at the same time. *~ Regan Murphy, The Review Team of Taylor Jones & Regan Murphy*

ACKNOWLEDGMENTS

Cover art by the author's granddaughter, Cheyenne Victoria Middleton

Poem, "In Dreams" from the author's book *Dreams of a Forgotten Man*

Poem, "Day's End" from the author's book *Dreams of a Forgotten Man*

Information on black bears: City of Aspen, Colorado website

Dreams Once Dreamed

Jack Sprouse

A Black Opal Books Publication

GENRE: ROMANCE/WOMEN'S FICTION

DREAMS ONCE DREAMED
Copyright © 2018 by Jack Sprouse
Cover Design by Cheyenne Victoria Middleton
All cover art copyright © 2018
All Rights Reserved
Print ISBN: 978-1-626948-79-2

First Publication: MARCH 2018

Published by Black Opal Books **http://www.blackopalbooks.com**

Dreams
Once
Dreamed

Chapter 1

The Bear

2002:

The campfire was burning low. One of the five campers, who were sitting around warming themselves, was ordered by the others to retrieve some more fire wood, lest the fire go out and leave them in the dark and cold.

"Come on, Grady, it's your turn," one of them yelled. "Go get some more wood."

"All right," Grady Nichols said.

He struggled off into the edge of the woods where they had cut and stacked a pile of fire wood earlier. He soon returned with an armload and placed a couple of logs on the fading flames. Soon it was blazing again. It was October, and they were in the high country on West Spanish Peak, so it was essential that they keep the fire blazing all night long. When the others went to their sleeping bags, Grady Nichols was the only one who had not been drinking beer. Grady had agreed to stay awake to keep feeding the fire. He wrapped himself in a blanket and poured some hot coffee. He put his feet right up against the fire and leaned back in his chair. The other four men were sleeping soundly, a couple of them snoring loudly enough to raise the dead, Grady was thinking.

About an hour later, he heard some rustling noise over at the edge of the woods where they had hanged the deer, that Rod Miller shot that afternoon. Rod had field dressed it, with the intention of strapping it to his truck the next morning and taking it home. Grady went to investigate. He took his flashlight. On his side, he carried a thirty-eight revolver.

As he drew closer to the spot where the deer was hanging, Grady heard grunting and more rustling in the leaves and grass. He shined his flashlight in that direction, and it reflected two yellowish eyes that turned and looked back at him.

"Oh, shit!" Grady yelled and started to back up.

It was a large brown bear standing up on its hind legs. It looked to be five or maybe six feet tall, and it appeared to Grady to weigh at least four or five hundred pounds. The bear lost interest in the deer and started moving toward Grady. Grady tried to yell for help, but fear and the cold prevented him from making sufficient noise to alert his friends.

Grady retreated quickly, all the time trying to draw his pistol from the holster. He lost his footing, stumbled backward, and fell. Screaming as loudly as he could, he got back to his feet and tried to run but turned to see where the bear was. He fumbled with the flashlight and pointed it in the direction of the bear.

The bear made up the ground between itself and Grady, and just as he made one mighty swipe at the man, Grady, terror stricken, got his .38 in his hand and fired at the bear, striking him in the shoulder. The bear's paw almost took the man's head off, but the pistol shot, that sent the bullet into him, woke up the other men. Their shouts caused the bear to head off into the forest and up the mountain.

The other men were up now and came running, only to find their friend lying there dead. They didn't panic but quickly wrapped his body in blankets and placed him in the back of their pickup truck. They then drove down the mountain to the small town of Cuchara, called for an ambulance and the state police. A trooper came and took their statements and then called the National Park Service to report on the bear.

"Gentlemen," the trooper told them, "we need you to wait here. The Park Service is sending a marksman to go after the bear. He'll want to talk to you about your location and get some details of what happened." The men agreed to wait after the ambulance picked up their friend Grady to take him to Pueblo for processing.

"I told them to have their man meet you guys at the corner of Colorado Twelve and City Avenue. So, if you guys can just hang tight, they said he'd be here in about an hour."

The bear that attacked Grady was brown in color, but it was a black bear. Black was a species, not a color. Many black bears were blond, cinnamon, or brown. Some of them were big enough to be mistaken for grizzlies, but there were few if any grizzlies in Southern Colorado.

The four men were noticeably shaken by the fate of their friend.

"One of us should have gone with him," Rod Miller said.

"Hell, Rodney, we would have if he'd woken us up," another one said. "Nobody even knew he was going out there."

They all nodded in agreement.

"Still, I hate to think how his wife is going to take this," Rod said.

It was about two hours before they heard a vehicle approaching from the south. They all turned to look and saw a National Park Services truck pulling into the street where they were waiting.

Out of the truck stepped a stern-looking man who appeared to be in his mid-thirties. He introduced himself as Jamie Cain. Cain looked to be about six feet tall and maybe a hundred-seventy-pounds. They all shook hands, and the man retrieved a notepad from his front seat. He took notes as the men began to describe their location and where they speculated that the bear had last been seen. It had happened in the middle of the night, so their information was sketchy at best, but the ranger seemed to be familiar with the area so he just nodded and thanked them.

"I'll go see if I can find him before he hurts someone else," the man said. Then he got back in his truck and left.

Cain drove back down Highway Twelve, the direction from which he'd come, to Cucharas Pass, and turned left on Route 364. This was a winding road that made a circuitous route up the West Peak. When he got to Cordova Pass, he spotted the deer the men had told him about. It was still hanging from the tree. There was a lot of blood on the ground about ten feet away from the deer, where the encounter had apparently taken place. A trail of blood leading off into the trees confirmed that the dead man had shot the bear, either right before or just as the bear hit him in the head.

Cain put on his heavier coat and retrieved his 308 Winchester from behind the seat, locked the truck, and began to follow the blood trail up the mountain. There were some signs that the bear was in distress. He had rolled over some brush and small trees and lost more blood. Cain was hoping he would find him already dead from bleeding out.

At this altitude, it was unlikely the bear would encounter any more campers or hunters, but Cain had to make sure.

About a mile above Echo Creek, Cain emerged from the tree line into a small meadow not far below the snow line. He could hear the roar of the wounded bear but couldn't see it yet. The roar sounded like it was a hundred yards or so away from his location. He peered through his binoculars and finally located the bear on the other side of the meadow. It was sitting against a rock, obviously in a lot of pain, and bleeding out from what appeared to Cain to be a shoulder wound.

Cain lay down on the ground, placed his rifle down in front of him, and sighted it in on the bear's head. His hand moved to the trigger guard, and his finger caressed the trigger gently. "Sorry, pal," he said out loud. "It's not your fault. Stupid men, stupid."

The crack of the rifle resounded throughout the little meadow. The bear slumped over backward and lay still. Cain walked over to where it lay just to make sure. It was a magnificent creature, he was thinking, such a waste of a great animal. Then he hiked back to his truck and drove down the mountain. He told the hunters they could go get their deer and their camping equipment. Then he radioed his report to the field office in Pueblo.

Cain lived in a cabin he'd bought in Beulah valley

along Highway 78 between Beulah, Colorado, and Pueblo. He was a private man and kept to himself, with few friends or acquaintances. He looked younger than his thirty-six years but only by a few years. He seemed to those people, who took the time to notice, to be carrying a heavy burden. Perhaps some tragedy had befallen him in the past, or he was troubled by a lost love or broken marriage.

He never talked about himself, so those who associated with him, on what might be considered a frequent basis, simply didn't know much about him. Cain's coworkers with the Park Service knew that he originally came from the Golden, Colorado, area and that his family was well off. Cain had been transferred from the Denver office in ninety-five to Pueblo, and he had been in that office since that time. He was an expert marksman and was the man they called on when that particular skill was needed.

Later that day, at his cabin, he brewed some coffee and sat down with a cup on the front deck, looking out over the mountains rising away from his property. His right hand held a picture frame, which contained a poem he had come across at an arts and crafts fair in Manitou Springs back in…1990? Maybe it was around that time. He couldn't remember exactly when it was.

The poem was called "In Dreams" and, as he gently rubbed his fingers over the glass covering the words, he withdrew deeper within himself and began to remember.

On the top of the poem, behind the glass, he had written a woman's name, *Abby*.

cʒeʒ

Cain drove to the Pueblo office to file an official report on the bear incident and to get his assignments for the coming week.

"What's your take on those hunters who had the encounter with that bear, Jamie?" the captain asked him.

"Inexperienced, Chief," Jamie responded. "They had a deer, field dressed and hanging up, just begging for some bear or mountain lion to come along and claim it. I think they were probably drunk."

"Well, it's a hell of a shame for a man to die like that just for being ignorant."

"And a bear, too."

"You're right. The bear was just doing what comes naturally. Anyway, thank you for taking him out. He might have killed someone else if you hadn't done it."

"No, he was dying when I found him," Jamie replied. "I just put him out of his misery."

"You did good."

"So, what do you have for me, next?" Jamie asked him.

"I need you to run up to The Springs and help them out. They've had a rash of unsafe campfires, and they could use your help tracking down some of the people doing it. We don't know if it's people deliberately trying to set the forest on fire or just idiots who don't know how to make a safe campfire to grill hot dogs."

❧❧❧

Jamie turned into Benny's convenience store, at Cimarron and Eighth Street in Colorado Springs, where he always stopped to get gas and a cup of coffee when he came through the city. He knew just about everyone who worked in the store and quite a few of the regular customers. The owner of the store, a man named Benny Morales, waited on him and ran his Park Service gas card to pay for the gas. "Coffee's on me, Jamie," he said.

"Oh, come on, Benny, you say that every time," Jamie replied. "Let me pay for one every once in a while."

"It don't cost me much. I appreciate the gas business."

Jamie shrugged. "Okay, well thanks again."

The front door of the store opened, and a young girl with red hair that fell almost to her shoulders came in and approached the register. Jamie was about to leave but stopped when he saw her and started watching her. She looked familiar to him—a beautiful girl, looked to be about sixteen. She was well-built, but that was not what attracted his interest. It was her mannerisms that drew his attention.

"I'm going to need ten dollars of gas on pump six," she told Benny.

He rang it up and, as she was paying him, she noticed Jamie staring at her and began to fidget.

"I'm sorry, miss," Jamie said, realizing that he made her nervous. "I didn't mean to stare at you. It's just that you remind me of someone I knew a long time ago."

"Oh, that's okay, sir," she replied. "I've been told I look like Julia Roberts, but I don't really believe it. Actually, I look like my mom."

Jamie smiled, but his heart started beating much more rapidly when she said that.

Just then, another kid, who was not with her, but apparently knew her, yelled loudly, "Hey, Jamie!"

Both Jamie and the girl turned quickly, said, "Yeah!" at the same time, then turned to look at each other incredulously.

"Is your name Jamie?" the girl asked him.

"It is," he said.

They both smiled and shook their heads in disbelief.

"Oh, my gosh, what are the odds on that?"

"Well, it's a dual-purpose name," he said. "I was named after my mother, but they had to call me James when we were together, so people would know which of us was which. But, yes, my name is Jamie."

She stared blankly at him for a moment. "Oh, my God, how weird is this? I was named after my dad. I never knew him. I mean, he disappeared before I was born, vanished in the mountains. They never found him. But my mother loved him, so she named me after him. She never stopped loving him."

Jamie was almost speechless. His chest was heaving, and his breathing became heavy. He was having trouble catching his breath. "Oh, my God, Abby, Abby?" Jamie uttered, to no one in particular, and grew dizzy.

He reached back to steady himself on the counter and knocked over a display rack that held sunglasses. The display fell to the floor, and Jamie fell with it. Benny hurried out from behind the register to see about him. The girl went to his other side and took his arm to help Benny get Jamie to his feet.

"Jamie," Benny called to him, "are you okay, buddy?"

After a minute or two, Jamie seemed to be clear headed and, with Benny and the girl helping him, he got to his feet. "I'm okay, thank you," he said.

"Here's some water," Benny said, handing him a cup.

Jamie took a sip and a deep breath, then he looked at the girl again. "What is your last name, miss?" he asked her after he regained his breathing.

She glanced at the name tag on his uniform that identified him as J Cain and started shaking and crying. "No, no, this can't be," she said, pushing away from him.

"It's okay, miss, I'm all right, I'm all right, don't worry, I'm okay," he told her."

"No, it's not that. It's your name tag. Your last name is Cain, sir, Jamie Cain was my dad's name. I think you're my dad."

Chapter 2

Abby

Eighteen Years Earlier:

The first day of senior year at Golden, Colorado, High School, Jamie Cain was depositing his books and other supplies in his locker. A girl with red hair, that fell just below her ears, walked up to the locker next to his, opened it, and put her books away. One look told him that this was not just an ordinary girl. The face was blessed with two amazing green eyes that looked to Jamie like they had the ability to make a guy do really silly things. Her lips were like a red valentine, what they called "tulip lips" that could draw a man's attention and hold it fixated on her mouth. She was beautiful and built like no female creature he'd ever seen. She was about to walk away when, feeling the desperation of the moment, he risked the humiliation of ridicule and rejection and stopped her.

"Hold up a minute there, precious," he said. "Where did you come from? I've never seen you around here. You can't just waltz in here and take my breath away then leave me alone, wondering if I dreamed you up or if you really happened."

"Wow," she replied, "does that stuff really work on the girls in this school?" She smiled mischievously and waited a moment to see how he would handle the question.

"Well, yeah, it has until now, but the girls in this school aren't widely known for their intellectual skills."

She began laughing and lightened up a bit toward him. She had not expected such a clever retort. "I'm Abigail Prentiss. My family just moved here from The Springs. My dad got a job at the Coors Brewery, so it was worth the move. I go by Abby. What's your name, handsome?"

"My name is Jamie Cain, but most people just call me handsome."

"Oh, do they, now?"

"No, they really don't. I made that up," he said.

"Well, you're a really good-looking guy, but you compensate for it with personality," she told him.

He started laughing.

"You didn't bring a boyfriend with you from The Springs, did you, Abby?"

"Nope," she said, "dumped him before I left."

"Oh, I bet he's hanged himself by now, somewhere up on Pikes Peak."

"No, I imagine he's found another fool by now," she replied.

"You sure don't talk like any fool I've ever known. There must be something I'm missing. You want to go get a burger and a coke with me after school? Maybe I can figure out what it is."

"I'll take a chance," she told him."

"Okay, great, wait for me here at the lockers, and we'll walk to my truck," he said.

"I'll have to call my mom and tell her I have a ride home. You can take me home later, can't you?"

"I'll take you to the moon as long as you let me tag along," he said.

"Don't stand me up, or I'll be mad."

"With that red hair, I don't ever want to take a chance on making you mad."

She giggled. "It's deceiving sometimes."

∽∾∽

After school, she was there at the lockers waiting for him, just like she said she would be.

They walked to the parking lot and got into his truck.

"Do you have a girlfriend?" she asked him.

"I'll have to let you know later this afternoon," he replied, and she started giggling. Her laugh was intoxicating to Jamie.

"No, I mean, besides me."

"Oh, besides you?" He feigned surprise. "No, Abby, I am currently without female entrapment."

"Oh, so you're telling me I have a chance with you?"

"I like your chances," he said, nodding his head.

He took her to a local drive-in, and they went inside.They ordered burgers and fries and a couple of soft drinks.

"So, what is your story?" he asked her. "You said your dad got a job at the brewery and that's why you moved to Golden. Were you born in The Springs?"

"No, I was born in Germany. My dad was in the air force, stationed in Germany. I was born at Ramstein Air Force Base. We moved to Colorado Springs when I was fourteen, and Daddy ended his career at Peterson Air Force Base. Thirty years in the service and then he worked part time at several different jobs. When he got the job at Coors, we moved here this past summer."

"Wow, you've had an interesting life. I've never been anywhere but Colorado, except for Maine. My mother is from Maine. My dad was in the navy, and he met my mom in Maine. They got married and moved back here. He's from Colorado originally. I was born in Lakewood in 'sixty-six."

"We're the same age then. What month were you born?" she asked him."

"I was born February fifteenth, the day after Valentine's Day," he said.

"I was born in March, so I'm one month younger than you are."

"That means I should be wiser, right?"

"Probably not," she countered.

"But it is significant. You do know what this means, don't you?"

"No, I don't know what this means, but I have a feeling you're going to tell me."

"It means our stars are aligned. We were meant for each other. There's nothing we can do about it, no use to fight it. You have to be my girlfriend, at least until you find somebody better."

She started giggling again."Well, okay, I've got nothing better to do for the time being."

〰〰〰

They started dating regularly. Their sudden coupling became the talk of the school, being as sudden as it was.

He reached across the seat of his truck and pinched her arm."You're like a dream, Abby."

"Ouch," she said. "What was that for?"

"I have to keep making sure you're real, and that I didn't dream you up."

"My gosh, do you ever stop with the bullshit? You're supposed to pinch yourself, by the way."

"It's really not bullshit, Abby. You're beautiful and smart, a heck of a lot smarter than I am. You're more than a match for me in wit and quick thinking. You always seem to know what I'm going to say before I say it. And, when you look deeply into my eyes, I feel like you're looking into my soul. I'm just trying to figure out why I was so lucky to be the guy with the locker next to yours on the first day of school. Why did God smile on me that day?"

"Maybe he did it for me," Abby said. "Maybe he smiled on 'me.' Did you ever think about that?"

He appeared to be thinking for a moment. "Yeah, that must be it," he said.

She laughed loudly, shook her head, and slapped him on his shoulder.

ဏသဏ

One night they were parked on top of Lookout Mountain, looking at the lights of Denver and talking. That is, he was talking, and she was listening and staring at him intently. He glanced at her and did a double take which made her giggle. He continued looking at her.

"What?" she said.

"I love you, Abby," he told her. "I've never loved anyone before, but I love you."

"Are you sure it's not just infatuation?" she said.

"I'm sure. Will you marry me?"

"If you're serious, yes, I will, but shouldn't we finish high school first?"

He started laughing. "I am serious, and, yes, we should finish high school first. And that's why I'm sure it's not just infatuation. You are smart enough to think ahead. Like I told you already, I've been working part time for the state forestry service since last year. Well, before I met you, I had planned to attend either Colorado State University or Colorado Mountain College for a degree in forestry and then apply to the National Park Service. But I think, now that I've met you, I can't be away for that long. I'm thinking I will just take some night classes at the School of Mines. They don't specialize in forestry but I can study environmental engineering, and that will help me in the Park Service. I don't make a piss-pot full of money, but I'll be able to take care of us after we get married. If all else fails, I can go to work for my dad."

Abby chuckled at his euphemistic linguistics. "How much money exactly is a piss-pot full?"

"It's a substantial amount," he offered.

"So, there's more to you than just fun and games, I see," she said. "I love you too, Jamie. I don't know how it happened so quickly, but it did. Yes, I want to marry you."

"I wasn't always like this, Abby," he told her. "For most of my school life I was just fun and games. Now, this is going to sound like bullshit, but that changed the first time I laid eyes on you."

"You're right," she said, "it does sound like bullshit, but I know it's not. No guy could put on an act as convincing as you have, for as long as you have, if it weren't real. I believe you because it happened for me too at that very same moment."

Jamie was not only surprised but dumbfounded by how quickly and how completely and deeply he had fallen in love with Abby Prentiss. It was like, one day she didn't exist, and the next day she was the prime mover in the rest of his life.

He took her to his home, in Coal Creek Canyon, to meet his family. Jamie's mother and sister fixed dinner, and the Cain family discovered that there was much more to this girl than just her outward appearance. She was genteel, cultured, and well-spoken, having been educated in American military schools abroad most of her life growing up.

But while being a self-aware and confident young woman, she made it obvious to them that she was just as "taken" with their son as he was with her. It was clear to Jamie's parents that the two of them were determined to share their lives together.

"I love them, Jamie. They're wonderful people," she told him as he was taking her home after dinner at his house.

"I'm glad you do, Abby. I'm sure they think you're too good for me."

"Oh, I don't believe that," she said.

"They might, once they get to know you better."

"No, I saw how they interacted with you. You're their pride and joy."

"No, that position is filled. My sister is the perfect one," he said.

"Well, we girls are usually the favorites."

"You're mine, that's for sure."

e/ɔe/ɔ

After graduation, Jamie went to work full time for the state forest service. His stated duties were to provide technical forestry assistance to landowners, assist in wild-fire mitigation, and help landowners achieve their forest management goals.

In reality, he cleared brush, planted seedlings, and spent many hours in classroom training, learning about how to prevent and control forest fires. It was good train-ing for his future plans of joining the National Park Ser-vice. Jamie's dad always said that the boy wanted to be a forest ranger all his life, and now he was on his way to realizing his goal.

He and Abby were driving around the streets of Golden one Saturday afternoon, just talking and looking for something to do.

"When do you get your 'Smokey Bear' hat?" Abby asked him.

"It's in the tool box. You want me to get it?"

"Yes," she said. "I want to get a picture of you in it. Okay?"

"Okay," he said, pulled over, retrieved his hat from his tool box, got back into the truck, and put it on his head. He then started driving down the road again. She got her camera out of her purse and snapped a couple of pictures of him.

"Why do you keep your work stuff in your personal vehicle?"

"Sometimes I draw a different truck at the station and sometimes I even go to a different station, so I just take my stuff with me."

"I see," she said. "Hey, it's Saturday, what's on the agenda for tonight?"

"My folks are out of town. I was planning to house-sit for them." He looked at her with a sly smile on his face and winked.

"Would you like some company?" she said.

"If you don't have any previous plans. I wouldn't want to impose on your private time."

"I'll have to check my itinerary, but I think I can make some space for you."

ഇരുള

In his room, he took her in his arms and kissed her with a desperation he'd never shown before. Then he stopped and held her close to him.

"Abby, we can wait until we're married if you want to."

"Do you want to wait, Jamie?" she asked him.

"No, I don't want to wait. I wanted to do it in the hall when we first met by our lockers, but now I want to do what is right in your eyes. You are smarter about these things than I am."

She suppressed the urge to start laughing and remained serious. "I don't want to wait any longer," she said.

ഇരുള

Later, they were lying on their sides in his bed just looking at each other. Both of them smiled at the other one, and then, in unison, they both yelled loudly with enormous glee and wrapped around each other in a mad, loving embrace. When their lips finally come apart, he took her face in his hands and looked at her, mesmerized. "My God, you are so beautiful," he said. "We're going to have to do this again sometime."

"How about right now?" she proposed, giving him a "come-on" look.

"Can I get a rain-check on that?"

"Well, I suppose so, if you don't feel up to it," she replied, looking disappointed.

"Thanks," he said. "Well, looks like the rain has let up, can I cash that check now."

She jumped across the bed into his arms. He grabbed her, rolled her over, and started kissing her all over again. She shrieked, giggled, and wrapped her arms around his neck.

☙❧☙

Later, she was looking around his room, while he took a shower. A rifle stood against the wall in one corner and a set of pistols hung on the opposite wall. "You have a lot of guns," she said.

"I'm a hunter," he told her. "I spend a lot of time in the high country."

"I've never shot a gun," Abby said.

"I'll teach you how to do it after we're married."

Jamie and Abby decided to get married in June of 1986. They were both twenty years old and had been going together for two years. They had wanted to get married in the summer of 1984, but Abby's parents, Mark and Jenny Prentiss, objected, claiming that they simply had not known each other long enough. The two relented and put off their plans until Jamie was established with the National Park Service. He applied for a full-time position early in 1985 and was hired on, full time, a short while later He was one of the youngest men ever to be hired in the National Park Service.

Abby went to work at Children's Hospital Colorado in Denver and began attending classes at the University of Denver. She rented a small apartment near her work so she and Jamie would have a place to meet without drawing the condescending judgement of her parents.

They went together to the Cains and informed them that they were going to get married, and the news was met with joy, love, and best wishes. Jamie's parents held a celebration for them. Jamie's sister and brother-in-law and their two kids came for the affair. Abby's parents were invited but declined, citing a previous engagement of some sort. Abby apologized profusely to Jamie's mom and dad, but she told Jamie later that her folks were just unsociable assholes.

"That's okay, darling," he said. "I'm not marrying them, I'm marrying you."

Abby was upset with her parents for not attending the dinner celebration of her pending marriage at the Cain home, and she told her mother.

"They went to a lot of trouble for me, Mother, and they already accept me like I'm their daughter. It seems to me the least you and Daddy could do was show up for the dinner."

"I'm sorry, Abby, I really am. Your dad went to the Coors Wellness Center for a checkup, and they did an

EKG. He's got some heart problems. He's pretty sick. That's why we didn't go to your party."

"Oh, no," Abby replied, "I didn't know. I'm so sorry. I hope Daddy's okay."

"Well, I'm afraid he's not," Jenny said. "I'm happy for you, Abby. Jamie seems like a fine boy, and I know he comes from a good family. Your dad and I are both happy for you. We're just worried about what we'll do if he can't work anymore."

"I won't abandon you, Mom. I'll help you out if it comes to that. Don't worry."

"Thank you, Abby, I know you will."

Abby called Jamie's mother and explained why her parents had not come to the celebration dinner. Mrs. Cain was gracious and told her that was quite all right and wished her the best for her father. She thanked Abby for straightening out her son who, "really needed to be straightened out for quite some time." She said Abby was just the girl who could do it. And she and his dad were grateful to Abby for taking on the task. They were ecstatic to have her in the family.

The next Saturday morning, Abby received a call from Jamie. "I have the weekend off, let's do something."

"What do you want to do?" Abby asked.

"Something 'you' want to do," he said.

"I want to go to the mountains."

"Okay. I'll pick you up in an hour."

In an hour, they were heading out I-70. Abby slid

over next to him, curled her left arm around his right arm, and leaned her head against his shoulder.

"Where are we going?"

"To the mountains," he said.

"I can see that, but where in the mountains?"

"We're going to Grand Junction."

"Oh, okay," she said, "what's in Grand Junction?"

"There's a restaurant in Grand Junction with a train track running all around the place, up on the wall near the ceiling, and every so often a model train comes running through. It whistles and smokes and chugs along. I just thought you might like to see it."

"I'd love to see it," Abby said. "We should have gotten married already, Jamie."

"Nah, I don't mind giving in to your parents' wishes. I guess I understand how they feel. I don't think we're too young, but if it makes them happy and makes them accept me more, I don't have a problem with waiting."

"How did your folks handle your sister's marriage to…what's his name again?"

"Evan, his name is Evan, and holy shit, that's a story I'll have to tell you some time."

"Why not tell me now?" she prodded him.

"You sure? It's some weird shit."

"Well, I'm sure now, if I wasn't before. Yes, tell me."

"Okay. Well, you see, Evan was raised in kind of a screwed-up family. He's a great guy. He became my best friend. We went on hunting trips together a few times. But Evan's old man was kind of weird. He never told Evan he loved him, not ever, not when he was growing up or when he got older. He had this goofy notion that people should demonstrate their love for each other and not have to say it all the time. If you constantly say it, it loses the meaning. At least that's what Evan's dad believed."

"Let me guess, Evan never told your sister he loved her," Abby said.

"That's right. And it almost drove her nuts. You see, we grew up in a home where our folks were always telling us they loved us. And Clare loved Evan and was always telling him. He loved her too. She could tell because he treated her like a queen. But he just never said it. Anyway," Jamie continued. "Evan got a job with a petroleum company and went to work in Indonesia for two-years. He had to stay two-years to get some tax breaks. He planned to save his money and build them a home in the mountains, which he did eventually. But that's not the best part."

"Then get to the best part," Abby teased him.

"I am," he said. "Not long before Evan was scheduled to come home, his crew was taken hostage by some Indonesian bandits and held for ransom. We learned about all this after he got back. They were held a long time and finally decided to try an escape plan."

Abby sat up straight and was genuinely attentive to the story now.

"But when they set the thing in motion, all hell broke loose, and the guards started shooting. Evan managed to get a rifle away from one guard and killed him and two others but not before they killed the rest of Evan's crew. We got the word that he was dead after five months of not knowing what had happened to him."

"Oh, my God," Abby said, her mouth wide open.

"Yeah, I told you it was some weird shit, but he got away. He got on a log and floated down a river. He got bitten by a snake, went into a coma, was rescued by a fisherman, and ended up in a hospital in Hawaii with his company people there. There had been a mix up and, somehow, they thought Evan was another guy, so when they found out who he really was, they made arrangements to get him back to Denver and get him a rental car.

"Now, another hitch in the story. Clare had been working for the Denver Police Department and this detective, who had been assigned to accompany her on interviews to protect her, well, he fell for her and kept asking her out and wouldn't take no for an answer. The final 'no' set him off. They met in an apartment building hallway, downtown, after finishing an interview, and he assaulted her. He grabbed her and started kissing her and pulling up her dress. She couldn't get loose, so she bit his lip, and he slapped her a couple of times. She kicked him in the balls, hauled ass back to the station, and told the chief. The detective lost his job and spent six months in jail."

"What a nightmare that must have been for you guys."

"Oh, but that's not the best part," he said.

"There's more?"

"Yes, you see, there was this fella named Jimmy, at our church. He met Clare when they were fourteen, and he fell in love with her. I guess you could say that Clare tolerated Jimmy. They dated in high school, she went to the prom with him. After she met Even, she totally forgot about Jimmy, but he never forgot about her. When Evan was 'killed—'" He made air quotes to emphasize Evan being killed. "—Jimmy started pursuing her again. He was a Harvard lawyer by this time and, eventually, she just decided that she has nothing to live for, so she agreed to marry Jimmy.

"The wedding was on a Saturday at one o'clock. I was taking a class at the state forestry service facility so I was at home, also because I couldn't stand the asshole. Anyway, about ten o'clock, I was at the breakfast nook table eating some cereal, the family is all at the church, and the doorbell rang. I went to the door and opened it, and there stood Evan. I almost passed out. He asked where Clare was, like he'd been out of town buying furniture or something.

"Of course, I told him we thought he was dead. I told him Clare was getting married. He asked me what time, and I told him she was getting married at one o'clock. He asked me what time it is now. I told him we had time, get in my truck. We hauled ass down the canyon road going just fast enough to keep from getting airborne. When I got out of the canyon, a state trooper came after me, and I raced him to the church. I got there first, but he was right on my tail. I stopped at the edge of the parking lot, and Evan and I got out and started running toward the front door of the church."

"What happened?" Abby asked.

"The wedding was over, and everybody was gone."

"Oh, no, you can't mean that, Jamie."

"No, I don't. We crashed through the front door, and Evan yells out 'stop the wedding, she can't marry him.'

"Well, the proverbial shit hit the proverbial fan. Turns out they had not said their vows yet. Evan told Clare he loved her. Clare started bawling. We busted up the wedding. And when we came out of the church, the trooper was still there. Evan and I went over to him, and I started explaining to him why we had to get to the church so quickly, to stop my sister from marrying Jimmy so she could marry Evan, the man she really loved. The guy let me off the hook."

"I'm going to need a nap after that," Abby said and let out a sigh of relief. "At least our wedding won't be as dramatic as all that.

"Then how about we spend the night in Vail, and you can get some rest."

"Are you serious? I'd love to stay in Vail. But we didn't bring any pajamas or change of clothes."

"I'm serious. We can sleep naked, and it's not like we've been rolling around in the dirt. I'll find a laundromat and take your clothes and wash them. Of course, you'll have to wait in the room naked until I get back."

"That's okay, I can wear the same clothes. Let's do it, Jamie. I'd love that."

"I've got a better idea," he told her. "My dad mentioned a place he's brought my mom a few times when they just want to get away. I wrote it down before we left. Let me see." He looked at a slip of paper on which he'd written directions. "I get off at Frontage Road and then turn at Lionshead Circle. It's on the right. Marriott Mountain Resort."

"Oh, my gosh, Jamie. That looks expensive," Abby said.

"It's a once -every-so-often thing. Besides, they have those fancy robes we can wear around the room so we don't have to walk around naked, although I think I might prefer that you walk around naked."

"I don't have to have this. Remember, my dad was an enlisted man. We didn't live in the lap of luxury."

"Maybe not, but you've got a hell of a lot more class than I do."

"Oh, I don't know about that, Jamie. You couldn't have been raised by your folks and not have some of their class rub off on you."

"I think my sister got all the class."

"You're a decent man, I wouldn't have fallen in love with you if you weren't," she told him.

"I really love you, Abby. I mean, this is the real deal with me. I can't imagine life without you."

"I know you love me. You've convinced me of that, and I love you too, I always will."

"I want to do this for you, come on."

"Okay, but you have to let me pay for it," she said.

"Absolutely not" he insisted.

"Okay, thank you, but I just want you to know that I don't require this sort of thing."

"I don't either, baby. I just require a life style with you in it."

ℰ∽ℰ∽

Later, after their romantic ardor was assuaged and they were drifting off to sleep, she called his name, "Jamie."

"Um huh," he mumbled.

"You don't snore, do you?"

"No, Abby, I don't snore."

"Good."

"But I fart sometimes."

"No problem, so do I."

ℰ∽ℰ∽

The next weekend she was at her parents' house and had to face the obligatory chastising for her staying overnight with a man instead of returning home from a day trip.

"I didn't spend the night with a 'man,' Daddy. I spent the night with my fiancé, the man I am engaged to marry, the man I would be married to now had I not deferred to your wishes and waited a year. You and Mom might as well accept that Jamie and I are sleeping together because we love each other, and we *are* going to get married in just a few months. That's why I rented an apartment. It wasn't just to be close to my job, it was so I could be close to Jamie."

"Well, I just don't think it's right," Mark said."

"I know you don't, Daddy, and I understand how you feel, but I wish you would try to understand how I feel."

"But we're Catholic," he replied.

"What the hell difference does that make? Would it be okay if I were a Baptist?"

She left, went back to her apartment, and waited to hear from Jamie. She was hoping to get together with him. The confrontation with her father had left her bummed out. But it was not to be. Jamie called her to tell her he had to make a trip out to the White River National Forest. "This is an all-of-a-sudden deal, and I didn't have any pre-warning about it. I wish I had time to come see you before I leave, but I just don't. I'll be gone four days. Don't worry."

"But I will worry," she told him. "I will always worry about you when you go off into the wild west."

"You're starting to sound like my mother," he said.

"I'll probably turn into your mother one day."

"Well, as long as you don't turn into my dad, I'm okay with that. I'll see you when I get back. I love you."

"Love you back," she said.

e/se/s

Jamie headed out I-70, driving through Vail, and turned south on Route 24. He had to meet his contact in Leadville. After passing Gilman, he was about halfway to Redcliff when he noticed some rocks sliding onto the highway. He slowed a bit to better assess the situation. There didn't seem to be any major slide, so he drove on. But just as he passed the point where he first observed the small rocks falling onto the road, a large boulder rolled past the front of his truck. He slammed on the brake to avoid hitting it.

An even larger rock and several others with it slammed into the back-quarter panel of the truck and pushed it over the guard rail, off the road, and into the ravine on the other side.

The truck began flipping over and over, end over end many times, popping the front windshield out and tossing Jamie out of the truck and into the water and rocks of Eagle River at the base of the hill.

His head hit a rock, knocking him unconscious.

The truck came to rest at the bottom of the ravine in a stand of deep heavy brush. Jamie floated to a bend in the river and was caught in some brush and rocks. He became conscious, managed to pull himself out of the water, and again lost consciousness.

A day later, a road crew came along and cleared the highway of the rock obstructions. The larger boulders had rolled completely across the road and into the ravine, landing on top of Jamie's truck.

Jamie eventually regained consciousness and crawled farther up the rise, away from the river, and into a field.

천 න ඟ

When he didn't show up after four days, Abby called his office and was told that they had not heard from him. She was told not to worry and that they would check with the office in Leadville and see what information they could gather.

When the Leadville office reported that Jamie had not shown up, mild panic ensued at the Denver office of the National Park Service. An all-out search was ordered, and Park Service employees from all over the state headed for the White River National Forest area. Eventually, the truck was found at the crash site, but there was no sign of Jamie Cain anywhere, no blood no evidence of an attack by a bear or some other animal, and no footsteps leading away from the crash site. It was a complete mystery.

Two rangers were sent to Jamie's parents' house to inform them. Jamie's mother called Abby and told her. Mrs. Cain offered to come and get her, but Abby said she would drive to the Cains' house. The Cains were frantic when Abby arrived, and Abby wasn't much better.

"They have to find him, Mrs. Cain. They have to. I don't want to live without Jamie."

"Let's not jump to conclusions, Abby. They have a lot of people out looking for him. He was not killed in the accident, and there were no signs of trauma at the scene. Let's just hope and pray they find him."

"We were going to get married in four months. Oh, God, what am I going to do?" She broke down completely.

Mrs. Cain got a pillow and a blanket and had Abby lie down on the couch. She covered her with the blanket, and Abby slept about four hours. When she awoke, she appeared to have forgotten where she was.

Will Cain came into the room and saw Abby lying there. "How is she doing?" he asked his wife.

"She's taking it pretty hard. I just hope they find him pretty soon. The longer it goes on, the more I fear for our boy."

"Let's not panic, darling. You know Jamie is as tough as they come. Don't give up hope."

೧൭೧

Two months went by, and Abby had almost given up hope. She became distraught, started taking off from work a lot, and began just lying around her apartment, crying all day long. She stopped putting on her makeup and doing her hair, believing there was no point in it anymore. The love of her life was gone, and she was almost at the point of thinking she didn't want to go on living.

In June, Abby's father collapsed and died from a heart attack on the job. Abby was almost too far gone to feel much more trauma. She had been very close to her dad, more so than to her mother. His loss was extremely painful for Abby, but her heart was so full of hurt there just didn't seem to be any room for more. She would discover that, in time, Mark Prentiss's death would visit her, and she would make room in her heart for the grief. But for the time being, she had to cope with the current tragedy that life had given her.

Abby's mother was now like a child to be looked after and taken care of. Her husband's air force pension, while helpful and consistent, would only supply their most basic needs. Abby would have to give up her apartment, move back into the house, and take her job more seriously.

She began having bouts of nausea in the morning, and it became a regular thing for a couple of weeks. It began to interfere with her work so she made an appointment with her doctor to get checked out.

"How long has this been going on, Abby?" the doctor asked her.

She explained to him what had happened to Jamie. "I've been feeling bad ever since then, of course, but for the last couple of weeks, I've been nauseous and dizzy quite a bit."

"In the mornings?"

"Yes, usually, but sometimes later in the day."

"Have you done a pregnancy test?"

"Oh, my God, no. You don't think I'm pregnant, do you?" Abby said.

"It's possible, dear," he said. "The symptoms sound like that might be the case. We'll run some tests to be sure. Would that be a problem for you now, given your situation?"

She started crying but was able to speak and shook her head. "No, Doctor," she said. "It would be wonderful. Jamie and I want to have children. We hadn't figured on starting this soon, but it's okay."

A short while later, the doctor returned to her room. His smile told Abby that she was indeed going to have baby. "You're about four months along, so you need to contact a pediatrician."

She started crying again before she was finished at the doctor's office.

When Abby told her mother about the baby, Jenny Prentiss became almost frantic.

"What are we going to do, Abby?"

"What do you mean?"

"I mean, how are we going to afford a baby. Shouldn't you consider getting an abortion? Babies are very expensive."

"Oh, you go to hell, Mother. I'm not going to kill Jamie's baby. I want this baby. It's all I have left of him."

"Then you should get his family to help you support it," Jenny said.

"I'm not going to do that either. They've lost their son. I'm not going to cause them any more trouble."

"Well, that makes no sense to me," her mother replied.

"Please don't ask me that again. I am not going to ask them for money. I want to leave here, Mother. I want to get away from bad memories, go somewhere else, and start over."

"But what about me, Abby? You won't leave me here alone, will you?"

"No, Mother, of course not. Why would you even ask me that? I want to get out of Colorado for a while. Can we do that?"

"Well, we could go stay with your Aunt Betty in Colby. It's very small town, but she has a big house. We could stay with her for a while. I don't think you'll be happy in such a little town, but she'd be glad to put us up, I know. She's been all alone since Charles died"

"I'm not going to be happy anywhere, Mother. I just

want to get out of here to someplace I can maybe forget my life here."

"Well, when would you want to move there? I got a notice from the landlord yesterday that the lease is up next month ,and he wants to know if we're going to re-new."

"Okay, tell him we don't want to renew the lease. I'll need to give two weeks' notice, so we'll spend the last two weeks in my apartment, and you can get your deposit back. I'll let the apartment go, make arrangements to pay any money due on the lease, and then we can go."

"I'll call Betty and let her know that we'll be com-ing. She called me when your dad died and told me again that I was welcome, but at the time I didn't have any idea that you'd be going too. I know it'll be all right, but I'm going to call her just the same."

"Whatever, Mother," Abby told her, brushing off her rambling. "Just do it."

"I'll tell the landlord we're not going to renew the lease. I'm ready to leave, too. This place reminds me of your father too much, anyway. It hurts just to be here. We have so much stuff to move. How are we going to do it?"

"I'll rent a U-Haul trailer and pull it with my car," Abby said "Start getting all your stuff packed up. Oh God, how can this be happening to me? How can I leave here? This is where we met. This is where we were going to spend our lives together. Oh God, my heart is broken."

Chapter 3

Lost Time

Slowly the light was coming to his eyes. *I must have hit my head,*" Jamie thought. *It hurts something awful. I wonder where I am. There's a truck lying on the other side of this ravine. It looks like it crashed down the slope. I've got a knot on my forehead. I've got to get to a road where I can get help.* He started crawling up the rocks, over the side of the slope, and into a field. He stopped to rest and lay still for a few minutes to catch his breath then started crawling again.

Nightfall came, and he fell asleep. The temperature was dropping dramatically overnight, and he had trouble sleeping. He awoke at first light.

Good thing I had my heavy coat on while I was driving, or I'd be dead by now. It feels like snow. I've got to get to a road before the snow falls, or I'm going to freeze to death. Got to get to my feet. Can't make any time crawling.

He tried to get to his feet but grew dizzy and fell down. Continuing to crawl, he came to a dirt road. *I'll wait here, need to rest a while anyway. I'm feeling dizzy again.* He was drifting in and out of consciousness. *What's that noise? It sounds like a vehicle. I have to get to the middle of this road.* He crawled out into the middle of the road and waited. The vehicle came right up to him and stopped.

It sounds like a pickup door opening and slamming shut. I hear footsteps. Someone is dragging me out of the road. No, they're dragging me to the back of the truck. Someone is talking, but I can't tell what they're saying. Sounds like a woman, an old woman. I'm being lifted up into the bed of a pickup truck, and now they're pushing me into the bed. The tailgate closed. The door opened and closed again. *Now they've started the engine.*

When he awoke, he was lying in a bed in a house and was comfortable and warm, but his head was still hurting.

"Who are you, young man?" an older person's voice asked him.

He didn't answer right away.

"Can you hear me?" the voice asked again. "Who are you?"

"I'm not sure." He mouthed the words, but no sound came out.

"What? Are you trying to talk? You want some water?"

Jamie nodded. The person left the room for a minute or two and returned with a glass of water, which Jamie gulped down very quickly. He reached into his pocket for his wallet, but it wasn't there. He looked up at the person behind the voice and saw an elderly woman who appeared to be at least seventy years old.

"I lost my wallet," he told her.

"That's okay, son, you don't owe me any money. What's your name?"

"I don't know," he said. "I mean, I can't remember right now."

"Do you know what happened to you?"

"I think my truck was pushed off the road by a rock slide. I was thrown out and ended up in a stream."

"That was probably Eagle River," she said.

"I crawled to where you found me. That's about all I remember. I don't know if I left my wallet in the truck, or if I lost it when I was thrown out. My clothes are torn up pretty badly from crawling. I might have lost my wallet somewhere along the way."

The woman nodded. "My name is Ona Mabry. I'm gonna look after you, but I can't take you to the hospital. They killed my husband in the hospital, and I ain't gonna be responsible for getting another man killed."

"Thank you for picking me up. There should be people looking for me, but I don't know who they would be. I hit my head pretty hard, and I just can't think clearly. It'll all come back to me soon, I'm sure."

"I have an extra bedroom you can stay in," Ona said. "You need to get some rest. You gotta be hungry, though. I'll make you some soup, okay?"

"Yes, ma'am," he said. "That sounds really good."

"Good," she said, "but now you listen to me. I'm a crack shot. They used to call me the Annie Oakley of Colorado. I once shot a crow on the fly with a thirty-eight revolver, so don't get no ideas."

"No, ma'am, Miss Ona. I'll mind my manners." He ate the soup, drifted off to sleep, and slept all afternoon until the next morning.

The next morning, it looked like the whole world was covered in snow. There was at least six feet of snow in the drifts.

"It's a good thing I got you in here when I did, or you'd be buried under the snow right now," Ona said.

"I'm grateful to you, ma'am," Jamie told her.

"Call me Ona, boy. I ain't no ma'am."

"Okay, Ona. Thank you for saving me."

"And you don't know who you are?"

"I'm trying to think what I was doing and where I was going."

"Well, it don't matter right now. We're ass-deep in snow, and we're gonna be here a while. Don't worry, though. I got enough food for the winter."

"I don't want to eat all your food. I'll pay you back as soon as I get back to where I belong."

"Can you shoot?" she asked him.

"I feel like I can. Do you mean, like a rifle, or a pistol?"

"A deer rifle. My husband used to keep us in deer meat, but I have a hard time getting close enough to them to get a good shot off. I can't see so good anymore."

"Let me see your rifle."

Ona left the room and came back in a moment, toting a rifle. "This was my husband's rifle," she said and handed it to Jamie.

He took it, and Ona noticed right away that he handled it like a hunter. "It's scoped Marlin three-thirty-six thirty-thirty. Yes, this is a good deer rifle."

"So, you must be a hunter, boy," Ona said. "When the weather clears a bit, we'll go out and see if you can shoot worth a damn."

He watched the woman putting logs on the fireplace. She was energetic for her age. She was wearing Levies, a flannel shirt, and a Vietnam bush hat—probably her husband's—over her gray hair. She looked to be Native American, most likely of Ute ancestry, he decided. She was congenial, easy to talk to, and seemed to be happy just to have someone around the house to converse with for a change.

If he could just remember why he was here, where he

was going, and, more importantly, who he was.

He was wearing some kind of uniform, but it didn't help him identify himself. The shirt was torn above the left pocket where it looked like a tag of some kind may have been ripped loose, either in the accident or as he was crawling away. Most likely, if that happened, it happened in the accident because, when he was crawling, he was wearing the coat, and it would have been unlikely that he would have torn his shirt with the coat covering it.

❧❧

It was two weeks before they could even leave the house and, even then, it was too muddy to drive the truck. They hiked to the edge of the nearest woods on Ona's property.

"They come right up in the yard now. It's like they know, since Jake died, that I can't hit the side of a barn, so they come up almost all the way to the house, just to piss me off."

"I thought you told me they called you the Annie Oakley of Colorado, shot a crow out of the air."

"Ah hell, boy, that was before I got to know you. I was afraid you might be one of those serial rapists or something."

He started laughing. "Crack shot, you said."

"Oh, hush," she told him, scoffing. "There's some rocks and fallen trees to set the rifle on over here." She led him to a spot in the trees, and the two of them waited until a big buck wandered onto her acreage. Ona started waving at Jamie and pointing. He put his finger over his mouth, indicating for her to remain quiet, and took aim. The rifle cracked, and the deer went down.

Ona was ecstatic and giggled like a schoolgirl. He cautioned her to be quiet again as he pointed at another deer, and she quieted herself down. He took aim again and brought down the second deer. They field dressed the two of them.

"I'll go get the truck," Ona said.

"It's too muddy, Ona," he said. "I can drag them to the house."

"Nah, it's got four-wheel drive." She walked back to the house and returned shortly thereafter with the truck. They loaded the two animals into the bed and drove them back to the smoke house.

"Damn, boy, you're a shooter all right. I'm gonna hate to see you go once we figure out who you are."

"I'll come back to see you from time to time, Ona. I must have had a reason for being around here. Maybe I'll figure it out soon, and I can drop in and see you when I come back for whatever reason I was here this time."

"I'd like that. I'm not usually very sociable, especially since Jake died, but I'd love to have you come back to see me."

"Do you recognize the uniform I was wearing when you found me on that road and picked me up?

"Uhm no, I can't say as I do," Ona lied. She knew he was wearing the uniform of a park ranger but, in order to find out his identity, she would have to take him to the ranger station in Leadville, and Ona was not ready to do that. She'd wait until spring and then drive him into town and tell them she couldn't get him there until the snow melted and the ground dried up.

ⓔⓢⓔⓢ

Jamie spent long hours racking his brain, trying to remember anything that might bring him back to his life. He assumed his ability to shoot the deer was reflexive. He had obviously been a skilled marksman because he didn't even have to think about making those two shots. He'd just aimed the rifle and fired. His hand and eye did the work. His mind had not been needed.

I must have a family somewhere. What are they thinking? Am I married, do I have kids? Are they wondering where Daddy is? How old am I? Damn, I'll go insane if I dwell on this very long. How does this happen to someone? How can a man just not know who he is? It makes no sense. There has to be somebody out there missing him. Thank God for this old woman, or I'd be buried in the snow right now, hard as a preacher's dick and not nearly as warm.

July came, and Ona told him that she could probably get him into Leadville and see if somebody could find out who he is. "I hate to see you leave me, boy. I've grown attached to you, but you don't belong to me. You got a mother somewhere who's probably worried shitless about you, and I need to try and get you back to where somebody can give you more help than I can."

Jamie nodded. "Okay, Ona, but let me stock up your smoke house before I go. That's the least I can do for all you've done for me. Hell, Ona, you saved my life."

"It's what people do out here. This is hard country, and people have to help people when they need it. You've helped me a lot, chopping wood, shootin' deer. And just talkin' to me."

"Go get the truck warmed up, and we'll get you some deer meat before I go." She had shown him how to fill up the propane tank on the truck from the 500-gallon propane tank Jake Mabry had installed some years before. So, Jamie filled up Ona's pickup truck, and they drove off into the woods.

Jamie had shot three deer and was moving his position to take down a fourth one when he heard footsteps in the snow behind him, and a man's voice called out, "Hold it right there, buddy, put down the rifle, and don't move. Put down the rifle."

Jamie turned slowly and saw two men in uniforms with pistols drawn and aimed at him. He slowly put the rifle down on the ground and put his hands up over his head.

"What the hell do you think you're doing?" one of the men asked him.

"Shooting deer," Jamie replied.

"It's not deer season, sir, and, besides, you've shot three deer, and you were just about to shoot another one."

Just then, Ona walked into the scene. "He was killing deer for me. He was stocking up my smoke house."

"Who are you, ma'am?" the man asked.

"I'm Ona Mabry, I live near here. This man was in an accident last February. I found him and took him to my house and took care of him. He's been keeping my smoke house stocked with meat."

The ranger turned to Jamie again. "What is your name, sir?"

"He don't know who he is," Ona said. "He cracked his head on a rock in the wreck, best as I can figure, and he don't remember nothin'."

The ranger looked perplexed for a moment, walked over to Jamie, and looked at him closely in the face. "Oh my God," he said.

"What?" Jamie asked.

The ranger was shaking his head and tears formed in his eyes. "You're Jamie Cain, sir. You're a marksman for the National Park Service. You're a park ranger. We've been looking for you for six months."

"That's why you can shoot like that," Ona said. "What did you say his name is, Ranger?"

"Jamie, Jamie Cain. He works out of the Denver office. We need to take him with us, ma'am. We'll need to come back and get a statement from you too if you don't mind."

"I don't mind. Just let me know how my boy is doing. I've got kinda attached to him."

"I'll do that personally, ma'am. Here's my card. I'm Ranger Roger Murphy." He handed her his business card.

She took it and tucked it in the pocket of her flannel shirt. The rangers took Jamie to their vehicle, drove back to Highway 24, rushed back up to Interstate 70, put on the emergency lights, and headed for Denver. Murphy got on his cell phone and called the Golden substation.

"Let me speak to the chief, please," he said when the receptionist answered. "This is Roger Murphy."

"Hey, Roger, what's up? Why are you calling me on your cell phone?" the chief asked.

"I didn't want to broadcast this on the air, Chief. You're not going to believe this, but Landon and I just found Jamie Cain in the White River Forest." There was silence on the other end of the line.

"Did you hear me, Chief?" Murphy said.

"Yeah, I heard, Roger. I'm trying to process. What is his condition, how is he? What happened? Forget all that. Don't try to explain anything to me now. Is he coherent?"

"Yes, he's coherent, but he took a nasty knock on the head in the accident. He appears to have amnesia."

"Okay, get him to the hospital. I'll meet you there.

I'll call ahead. Take him to Saint Anthony—hang on a second."

Murphy heard the chief flipping pages in his Rolodex. "It's on West Second Place in Lakewood," the chief said. "Eleven-six-hundred is the address."

"I know where Saint Anthony is," Roger said. "See you there, Chief. Oh, one more thing, Chief, call his parents."

"Will do, Roger, thanks." He informed the rest of the staff at the station, and a cheer went up. He asked one of the women to call the hospital and tell them a crew was coming in with a patient, with possible amnesia, for evaluation. He looked through the computer files for Jamie's home phone number. He found the Cains' number and his fingers trembled as he started dialing.

"Please, answer," he said out loud, as the phone rang twice then three times. Finally, someone picked up the receiver.

"Hello," a woman said.

"Yes, is this Mrs. Cain?"

"It is."

"Mrs. Cain, this is Chief Green from the National Park Service. Two of my men just located Jamie in the White River Forest and are taking him to St Anthony Hospital in Lakewood."

"Oh my God!" she screamed. "Do you mean it, how is he? Is he okay? What happened?"

"Ma'am, I don't know his condition. My ranger says

he is well, physically, but appears to have amnesia. We won't know until he's evaluated. They're taking him to Saint Anthony Hospital in Lakewood. I am going to head over there in just a few minutes."

"I'm going to call my husband, and we'll be there, too," she said. "Thank you, Chief Green, thank you so much."

The chief was at the hospital when Murphy and Smith arrived with Jamie. The emergency staff brought him into a room; prepped him with an IV and monitoring devices; took blood his pressure, heart rate, and etc.; and made him comfortable. The chief told him he was not going to question him until the doctors had a chance to look at him and do some tests. He met Jamie's parents in the hall outside Jamie's room. They were anxious to see their son, as was to be expected. A neurologist approached them and asked them to accompany him to a nearby office. When they had sat down, he introduced himself and explained Jamie's condition to them briefly.

"I'm Doctor Petroski, Mr. and Mrs. Cain. Your son has experienced some trauma to the head. Here's what we are going to do first with you two. Now, don't take this wrong, but I have to say it. Some individuals fake these events, and I don't, for a minute, believe that your son is faking his amnesia, but we always have to eliminate that possibility. There's a simple way to do it. We'll have him hooked up to equipment to monitor all his vital signs. We will observe Jamie when you are brought into the room.

Jamie's reaction to you will tell us if he is in a true amne-
siac condition or if he's faking it."

The Cains agreed. They understood that they would
simply be brought into the room with no introduction or
explanation and asked to approach the bed where Jamie
was lying. Several doctors and a couple of nurses were in
the room, monitoring the various pieces of equipment,
and talking to Jamie, when his mom and dad appeared at
the door with Doctor Petroski. The doctor accompanied
them over to the side of their son's bed. Jamie made no
reaction as his mother and father stood there looking at
him. None of the vital -sign monitors signaled any change
in his heartbeat or respiratory levels. He did not recognize
his parents.

Then the inevitable happened, his mother broke
down and started crying. She put her face in her hands
and wept uncontrollably.

Jamie was visibly moved by her emotional trauma.
He reached for her hand and took it in his. She held on to
his tightly. "I'm sorry, ma'am. I know you must be my
parents, and I know I should recognize you, but I just
don't. I'm sorry. I wish I could, I really do."

"It's okay, honey," his dad said to Jamie's mother.
"James had a nasty blow to his head. It'll all come back
to him in time."

The heartbeat monitor started registering increased
activity. Jamie began breathing harder, and his chest was
heaving in and out.

"Something's happening, Doctor, his pulse rate just went up," a nurse said.

"You called me James," Jamie said, pointing at his mother. "You always call me James because I have the same name as my mom."

Nothing short of pandemonium broke out in his room. His mother started crying again, and both parents hugged him. He hugged them back but offered no indication that he fully remembered them. The doctor determined that the one trigger, his dad's saying Jamie's alternate name, might have begun a slow process of recovery. It was a hopeful beginning.

Doctor Petroski decided that a trip to his home might be helpful, so he asked that Jamie's parents let the doctor follow them and drive Jamie to their house in the mountains. The Cains agreed. Along the way, Jamie seemed to recognize some of the landmarks but not to any degree that evoked a tremendous amount of emotional change in his demeanor.

When they pulled into the driveway of the Cain family home, he exhibited more interest.

Once inside the house, Jamie seemed more comfortable and immediately began walking down the hallway toward his bedroom. The doctor and the two parents remained silent and just watched to see what he did. They heard a door open and shut. Will Cain walked over to the hallway and looked.

"I think he went into his room."

"Let's just wait and see what he does," the doctor said.

They heard the door open and shut again, and Jamie came walking back out into the living room.

"My rifle needs cleaning, Pop, how long have I been gone?" he said.

The three of them looked at each other in bewilderment.

Finally, his dad spoke. "I meant to clean the rifle while you were gone, son, I apologize. I've been busy. I'll get on it next week."

"Don't worry about it," Jamie said. "I'll do it as soon as they let me come back home."

His mother started crying again, and the doctor smiled widely. "How are you feeling, James?" he asked him, calling him by the name his parents used at home.

"I want my mom and dad to meet Ona," Jamie said.

"And who is Ona, darling?" his mother asked.

"The lady who saved me. She found me in the wilderness, took me to her home, and took care of me. I wouldn't be here if it weren't for Ona."

"Well then, we definitely should meet Ona," his dad said. "Can that be arranged, Doctor?"

"I'm sure it can," Petroski replied. "I'll talk to Chief Green about it."

"Thank you, Doctor," Mrs. Cain said.

Doctor Petroski asked Jamie to wait in his car while he talked to his parents for a few minutes. Jamie nodded his head, walked over to his mom and hugged her. "I love you, Mom. I'm sorry I didn't recognize you at the hospital."

"That's all right, darling, I'm just glad to have you back."

He then hugged his dad and went out to Petroski's car.

"This is wonderful, folks," Petroski said. "So amazing that just walking into his house brought so much of his life back to him. This is a good case study."

"Doctor, there's one other thing," Mrs. Cain said. "Jamie went into his room, and in his room, there are pictures of the girl he was going to marry. He never mentioned her when he came out."

Petroski looked puzzled. "Well, we just never know how this thing is going to work in different people. I suppose it's possible that he didn't notice them but that's doubtful. You say they were going to be married."

"Yes, they were insanely crazy about each other. Abby, that's the girl, came here a couple of times after Jamie went missing. She was not handling it well. We were starting to worry about her. She looked pretty awful the last time we saw her. Then, to make things worse, a short while later, her father passed away. I was worried that she might do something to herself. The last time I went to her house, she and her mother were gone. The landlord was there and said they left no forwarding address. He gave them their deposit back because they had been good renters for several years. We didn't know where to look for her. She just disappeared."

"Well, I wouldn't mention her to Jamie," Petroski said. "It might trigger some negative emotion we don't want to have to deal with right now."

"Should we take down the pictures?"

"No, he might notice that they're gone. Just leave everything as it is. This has been a good day. Perhaps we'll have more good days very soon."

"Thank you for your help, Doctor," they both told him.

On the trip back to the hospital, Doctor Petroski asked Jamie a few questions. "So, you're a hunter, are you, Jamie."

"Yessir, Doc," he replied. "I've been hunting since I was a kid."

"Your dad taught you how to hunt?"

"No, my grandpa, Bill. He was a great hunter, and my grandpa Richard too, he's my mother's dad. They were the hunters in the family."

Doctor Petroski contacted Chief Green and informed him that Jamie had remembered his folks and wanted them to meet Ona Mabry, the woman who had rescued him.

The chief agreed that it was a good idea, and he dispatched Roger Murphy to retrieve the cantankerous old woman. The approximate time of her arrival at the hospital was calculated, and a call was made to Jamie's parents. They showed up at his room just a short while before Ona arrived with Roger.

Ona caused quite a stir when she walked down the hospital corridor. She was about the closest thing to a mountain man anybody had seen in Colorado in at least eighty years or so.

She and Roger Murphy were laughing about how he had caught Jamie shooting deer out of deer season. As they walked into Jamie's room, they seemed not to notice that his parents were already there.

Roger was extolling the skills of Jamie Cain as a marksman. "I tell you, Ona, Jamie Cain can put a bullet in a deer's eye at two-hundred yards."

"Two hunnert yards? What the hell are you talking about, Roger Murphy? At two-hunnert yards, that boy could put a bullet up a deer's asshole and make it come 'out' its eye."

The room filled with laughter, and Ona noticed the man and woman standing there next to Jamie' bed.

"Oops, I gotta learn when to keep my mouth shut," she said. "You must be the boy's folks. He looks like you."

"We are, Ona," Will said. "And we're honored to meet you. Thank you for saving our son's life." They both hugged her tightly, and Ona was taken by surprise. She had not expected two 'city slickers' to get that close to her.

"He's a mighty fine boy. He helped me out a lot the

time he was with me. I hated to see him go, but I know you are awful happy to have him back."

"We are, Ona, and he wouldn't be here if it weren't for you. We'll always be in your debt."

"Aw, no, you won't. It was just a natural thing. I had to help him. He wudda died if I didn't. How could I not help someone in trouble like that? It ain't Christian."

"When I get back to work I'm going to look in on you from time to time, Ona," Jamie told her. "That is, if you don't mind."

"I don't mind," she said. "I'd like that. Just remember to bring your deer rifle."

"So, when can I go back to work, Chief?"

"I'm afraid the doctors are going to have the last word on that, Jamie," the chief said.

The specialists were not sufficiently confident that Jamie was ready to be released back into the world.

"His recovery is indeed remarkable," one of them told Doctor Petroski. "He knows his parents, his coworkers, and he seems to be able to function capably. But what if he gets off by himself and has a relapse? We just need more time to determine for sure if he's ready. Keep in mind, there is the case of this girl he was going to marry. He has never mentioned her, according to his parents. What if, all of a sudden, she comes back to him—to his mind, I mean. It could throw him into a whole new dimension. We just don't know what damage that might cause."

"Okay, I have to defer to your expertise," Petroski said. "You'll keep him until you're comfortable with releasing him."

It was the Summer of 1987, when Jamie left the hospital and went back to work with the Natioanl Park Service. He was weak in his legs and arms from lying in a hospital bed for so long, even though the staff had put him through a physical therapy routine every day.

He began lifting weights at home every day and jogging up and down the canyon road. After a few weeks, he felt his former strength returning.

His parents were astounded that he walked past Abby's pictures on his wall every day, many times a day, and never once mentioned her or asked them who the girl in the picture was.

The human mind was a strange and complex organ that was beyond the ability of any human to fully comprehend. His mother wondered if she took down the pictures, would even notice, but she dared not take the chance.

She held out hope that one day he would return to his full mental capacity, and, before she went to sleep every night, she prayed for him. She also prayed for the mysterious girl who had disappeared from their lives so completely and so quickly, that she was alive and well and that one day Jamie would find her and love her again.

Chapter 4

Starting Over

Colby, Kansas, was only 235 miles from Denver, but it was like a whole different world to Abby. Colby was a small town of barely 5,000 people. Jenny Prentiss's sister, Betty McBride, a widow, lived in a house on Garfield Avenue in Colby. She had lived there with her husband Charles McBride for twenty-eight years until his death in 1982. Her house was paid for, and she lived off of her husband's retirement pension. She managed to get by fairly well financially, but Betty was a very lonely woman.

Being only fifty years old, and having been married to an older man for most of her adult life, she was beginning to feel that life was passing her by. When her younger sister, Jenny, called and asked if she and her daughter could come and stay with her a while, Betty was thrilled.

She saw it as an opportunity to have other people around and maybe get out "on the town" a bit. She would be a bit disappointed to discover that her twenty-year-old niece had no interest in partying. But rather, she was coming to Colby to forget everything in her life and to try to make a new life for herself and for the child growing inside her.

The first thing Abby did, when she got settled into her Aunt Betty's house, was to contact a local pediatrician and make an appointment. She also went to the county assistance office and applied for help with her pregnancy expenses.

Her doctor, Kevin Martin, was an older man with a calm and caring nature.

Abby explained her situation to him after he asked her if she was suffering with depression. "Yes, yes, a bit," she responded and told him about Jamie.

"There is a gentleman who teaches at the Community College, who has a grief counseling seminar, so to speak, once a week. It's a group thing, made up of several people who have lost loved ones. You might be interested in attending the seminar. I've heard he has helped quite a few people."

"Perhaps after my baby comes, I might look into

that. I don't know if I can handle it right now, Doctor, but thank you," Abby said.

"Well, I'll give you one of his cards in case you change your mind."

Abby studied the card the doctor gave her, trying to imagine what Lew Morgan looked like and how he counseled people who had lost loved ones. Did he tell them they would see their lost love or parent or child in heaven one day? She used to believe that, or at least she thought she did.

Now, she wasn't sure if she ever believed it or not. She had met the love of her life when she was eighteen-years-old. She knew he was the love of her life within two minutes of meeting him, and then he was gone, just like he'd never been there. Now she was carrying his son or daughter. God was merciful sometimes. She would have a piece of Jamie left to hold onto, for a while at least.

A child was forever but was not with you forever. One day the child would meet someone, leave you, and go away. Then you would be alone again.

She had already decided that she would name the baby Jamie, whether it was a boy or a girl. The name being appropriate for either gender made it easy for her to select it. If it turned out to be a girl, she would name her Jamie Lynn, after Jamie's mother. Jamie had been named after his mother, and his daughter or son would be named after his or her father.

It's just a happy twist of fate, Abby thought. Her only prayer, if her nightly plunges into self-pity could be called prayer, was that her baby would be strong and healthy and able to take on the world on his or her own, stronger than Abby had become of late.

Their need for money eventually overrode her need to feel sorry for herself, so she applied for a job at the local hospital as a nurse's aide. Her experience at Children's Hospital Colorado, and having earned her Certified Medical Assistant "CMA" license at the University of Denver, helped her get the job.

They hired her at part time because of her condition, with the promise of putting her on full time after her baby was born.

The extra money coming in made life much easier for her and her mother, and her Aunt Betty was so happy to have people around that she encouraged them to stay with her as long as they wanted.

Doctor Martin, noticed that Abby's demeanor had lightened up a bit and asked her about herself. "You seem in better spirits, Abby," he said. "How are you getting along?"

"A little better, Doctor," she told him. "I got a job at the hospital. It's only part time, which is best, I suppose. But they tell me I can work full time after the baby comes. I guess it will be after I recover from the birthing, a few weeks probably."

"That's good news. I'm happy for you. I saw the report. It looks like your baby is healthy. I'm sure you're happy about that."

"I am happy. I just wish its dad were alive to see him or her grow up and turn into whatever he or she will become."

"I know," he said sadly. "Life is tragic sometimes. I wish you would think about that grief counseling thing I mentioned. I'm told that young man is pretty helpful to a lot of people."

"I will, Doctor," Abby said. "I mean it. I'll give him a call."

"I hope you do. I think it will help you."

ဢသဢ

The voice on the phone sounded masculine but gentle, which would have seemed to be a contradiction in terms to Abby, before she met Jamie. As she had done when the doctor gave her the man's business card, she tried to imagine what he looked like from the tone of his voice.

"Yes," she said. "My name is Abigail Prentiss, but I'm called Abby. I got your card from Doctor Kevin Martin, my pediatrician. I'd like to discuss attending your grief counselling sessions."

"Certainly, ma'am. The sessions are on Thursday night from eight to ten. Do you know where the community college is?"

"I'll be able to find it, I'm sure. The town is not that big."

"No, it isn't," he said. "Do you live in Colby?"

"I've just moved here with my mother. We're staying with my aunt at her house on Garfield Avenue. I'm working part time at the hospital."

"Okay, I'll give you the building number and room before we hang up but first, let me ask you a couple of questions, if you don't mind."

"No, not at all, go ahead," she replied.

"First, will you have any problem discussing your situation with me and maybe two or three other people?"

"No, I don't think I will. I may be a little nervous."

"Nervous is okay. Just keep in mind that everyone there is in a similar situation and state of mind as you are."

"I'll try and keep that in mind. I see that from your card that you're a professor. What's your title, Mr. Morgan?"

"Lew, is my title, Abby, call me Lew."

"Oh, okay." She chuckled at his genuineness. "Thank you, Lew. I will see you Thursday at eight."

"I look forward to meeting you, Abby," he told her.

❧❧❧

Abby and her mother went to church with Betty on Sunday. Betty attended Grace Baptist Church in Colby.

Abby's mom and dad had been Catholic, and Abby had always gone to church with them. She even had her confirmation when she turned twelve. But, in their later years, Abby's parents had drifted away from the church, and Abby had not been forced to continue her participation. The family did their annual obligatory Midnight Mass on Christmas, but that had become pretty much the extent of their religious life as Abby grew into her teenage years.

The Cains were Methodists, but Jamie only went to church with them on the rare occasions when he had no other plans. So, when Aunt Betty asked them to go to church with her, Abby had no good reason to decline.

She found the music comforting, soothing, and almost renewing, unlike what she remembered in her days of going to Mass. The Mass had been more regal somehow, and authoritarian. She had felt like God himself was directing the Mass and that all of heaven was in attendance. But that was when she was twelve years old. This church seemed more personal to Abby. The music spoke of salvation and eternity flying away on the wings of angels. She didn't really understand it all, but she enjoyed the service. The preacher yelled too loudly on occasion, but he seemed nice enough, and the choir sang some very pretty songs. She told her Aunt Betty she wouldn't mind coming back sometime.

They were giving her desk work at the hospital. She was typing up reports and arranging files. She sat in a chair with casters so she could roll from her desk to the file cabinet and not have to get on her feet to file something. The head nurse, a woman named Mattie Summers, had taken Abby under her wing, so to speak, and had assured her that she would be able to work as long as she possibly could, right up until the baby was due. Mattie was a slightly overweight, congenial black woman who always seemed to be smiling. She wore a cross on a chain, around her neck. Mattie had pictures of all her children and her husband on her desk. She took an instant liking to Abby and did her best to make things easy for the young woman.

"Don't you worry about your job, Abby," Mattie told her. "It'll be here as soon as you're able to come back to work. Just don't think you have to rush right back in a week and hurt yourself."

"Thank you, Mattie," Abby replied. "Everyone here has been so nice to me."

"That's small-town ways, honey. Everybody knows everybody, and we all try to look out for each other."

"I appreciate what you've done for me. Thank you."

"You're welcome. Don't mention it," Mattie said. "It's no big deal."

Thursday night at eight o'clock, Abby arrived at the community college and found the building number Lew Morgan had given her. She parked her car, went in, found the room, and, upon entering, saw him sitting at a desk at the front. He stood up when he saw her. He was a nice-looking man, about the same height and weight as Jamie was, only with a slight paunch in front, that was, undoubtedly, due to his more sedate profession.

"You must be Abby," he said and reached out to shake her hand.

She offered hers, and they exchanged handshakes.

"I am," she said, "and I guess it's safe to assume that you're Lew."

"Yes, it is safe to make that assumption. So, I see you are going to have a baby. Are you hoping for a boy or a girl?"

"I'm okay with a boy or a girl," Abby said. "I just hope it's healthy and smart."

"Boy or girl, one of my two favorites," he said, and she laughed. She had a pleasant, endearing laugh, he noticed.

"Have a seat, Abby. The others will be along directly. We have three others, usually, but one of them is sometimes erratic."

Shortly, three more people came through the door, and each of them acknowledged Abby. She then found a seat and sat down. Lew stood up and lifted his coffee cup.

"I made some fresh coffee if anyone wants a cup. It's in the back. If not, then we'll get started. We have a new person with us tonight, so I think, if you all don't mind, we'll each stand up, introduce ourselves, and explain briefly why we are here and what we hope to gain from our time here. Cynthia, will you please begin."

A blonde-haired woman stood up. She was visibly nervous, and her voice quavered a bit as she began to speak. "My name is Cynthia Ellison, and I live in Colby. About six months ago my baby died. We don't know why he died, he just died. They called it SIDS, sudden infant death syndrome. They keep telling me that it will get easier as time goes by, but it hasn't yet. I guess what I hope to get from these sessions is some understanding of why it happened, if that's possible."

"Okay, Cynthia, thank you," Lew said. "Brent?"

A young man about twenty-five stood up. "I'm Brent Dawson and my wife, Joyce, was killed in a car wreck about a year ago. I miss her so much that, sometimes, I think I just want to put a bullet in my head, but I know I shouldn't do that. I'm just looking for a way to want to go on."

Mary Parker told a similar story of losing her husband in a construction site accident and not wanting to go on without him. Then Lew asked Abby to stand up and tell them about her situation.

"My name is Abigail Prentiss and, as you can see, I am going to have a baby. It's due in November, and I'm looking forward to meeting him or her. But, obviously, that is not why I'm here. I met my baby's daddy, the love of my life, in high school, in our senior year in Golden, Colorado. It was instant love at first sight for both of us. We went together for two years and were planning to marry this past June."

"His name was Jamie, and I plan to name our child after him, boy or girl. He worked for the National Park Service, he was a park ranger, and he was on an assignment when his truck was knocked off the road by a rock slide. He was thrown from the vehicle and apparently either killed or injured and died in a winter storm or was dragged of by an animal. They never found him." She started to tear up as she told the story. "I'm sorry. Anyway, a short while after that my dad passed away and staying in Colorado was just too painful for both me and my mother, so we came to Colby and moved in with my mother's sister, my Aunt Betty. I guess I hope to learn how to cope with not having him around every day. The pain is almost unbearable."

Lew cleared his throat. "Okay, I want to thank you all. I know it's not easy discussing such painful memories. It isn't easy for me either. I lost my wife Peggy to cancer three years ago and there's not a day that goes by that I don't try to pretend she will still be there when I go home in the afternoon. Peggy was my soul mate, the love of my life. I won't ever get over her, not completely.

"You can remember those you loved with fondness and love. Don't try to forget them. But you must try to recover that part of *you* that you lost when you lost them. That's what you're missing. When your loved one went away, they took part of you with them. Until you get that part of you back, you can never heal."

❧❦❧

After the third session, Abby discovered that she was enjoying the sessions, even if she was not convinced they were relieving her heartache over Jamie. Lew looked at her with a mixture of emotions that she read as both sincere compassion and some degree of desire.

For him, even her sorrow and her disfigured body could not hide the beauty of her face. She was still pleasant to look at, and her eyes still held the promise of something more for a man to contemplate. She began catching Lew staring at her face and her eyes with more and more interest, the longer they were around each other. One evening, he called her and asked her out to dinner.

"Are you sure you want to be seen out in public with a pregnant woman, Lew?" she asked him.

"That's the part of you I admire the most, Abby. I would be honored to take you and your baby out to dinner if you can afford me the time."

"I would enjoy that, Lew, thank you."

Lew and Abby continued having dinner out occasionally, and she decided it would be a nice gesture to fix dinner for him at the house one evening when Betty and her mother were going to a function at the church.

Abby did not fancy herself a great cook, but her Aunt Betty was. Aunt Betty helped her prepare a roast, some baked vegetables, and a great cherry jubilee desert before Betty and Jenny left for church and before Lew arrived at the house.

"Wow, Abby," Lew said after they began eating. "This is really great food. What a pleasant surprise. You're beautiful and a good cook too."

"I have a confession to make, Lew. My Aunt Betty helped me with dinner. I can cook, but I'm not as good a cook as she is."

"Oh, that's okay. My Peggy was not a great cook. She tried hard. She was always trying new recipes, and every so often she came up with a really good dish. We ate out a lot."

"Do you have a picture of her?"

"I don't carry one with me anymore. I have some at home, of course, but they're put away. It was just too painful to see her face on every wall in the house."

Abby nodded in understanding. "I've been meaning to ask you, what do you teach at the college?"

"I'm a psychology professor, if you can believe that."

"I don't have a problem believing that," Abby said. "You seem very smart."

"Educated maybe, I don't know how smart I am."

"Oh, come on. The grief counselling class did me a lot of good."

"Did it?

"Yes, it really did," she said. "I learned a lot about myself. I don't think I'll ever get over Jamie, but I think I'll be able to cope. I'm going to have a child now, so I have to think about that more than about myself."

"Yes, you do, Abby, and that brings up something I want to talk to you about. Please hear me out before you react, either positively or negatively. We're in similar situations. I lost the love of my life, and you just told me you don't think you'll ever get over Jamie. Peggy and I wanted children more than anything in the world. We discovered that I can't—have children, that is—and with her gone, I'll never be able to adopt." Abby was growing more and more curious where he was going with this conversation.

"Aw, hell, Abby, a blind man can see how I feel about you. You have to know that I care about you very much, and I love your baby too, even though I don't even know what it is yet. I love you, Abby. If you will marry me, I'll take care of you and the baby, and I'll be good to you both. I don't pretend that I can ever take the place of the one you lost, but we can be a family. Jamie will have a stepdad, and I'll treat it like it's my own."

"But are you sure this is what you want, Lew? It hasn't been that long since you lost your wife."

"Yes, I'm sure. I would never have even looked in that direction if I hadn't met you and your baby. But now, one more thing, and this is important. I hope this is not a deal killer for you. You have to realize that, even though I can't have children, I am a normal man otherwise. I'm not proposing a platonic relationship. I mean, you *are* a beautiful woman, Abby, and no man could look into those beautiful green eyes and not think about—"

She interrupted him. "I won't marry a man who doesn't want to have sex with me, Lew."

"Okay, well, I guess that settles that. So, will you marry me, Abby?"

"Yes, Lew, Jamie and I will marry you. I just need for you to understand that I want him to know about his father as he grows up. I want to tell him who he was and what happened to him."

"Of course, Abby. I don't have a problem with that. You loved him. You'll always love him, just as I'll always love Peggy. Of course Jamie should know who his father was."

☙❧☙

It was a simple ceremony at Grace Baptist church. Abby was showing, but no one seemed to notice. Neither of them wanted a big affair. Jenny Prentiss was surprised that Abby had decided to marry so relatively soon after losing Jamie, but she was hopeful that her daughter would finally find happiness.

Abby moved into Lew's house on Cherry Street in Colby. It was a much nicer house than Aunt Betty's and, with Abby gone, there was more room for Jenny and Betty.

When a baby girl came on November twenty-fourth, Lew was at the hospital with Abby. He was at the nursery window, showing the baby to people. After all, he was the girl's stepfather.

At her bedside, Lew fawned over the baby and continually asked Abby if she needed anything. Aunt Betty and Jenny Prentiss both smiled knowingly and, once, when Lew left to go downstairs to the cafeteria, Betty told Abby, "That man is really in love with you."

"It's not that, so much," Abby said. "He and his wife could not have children. He always wanted them, but she never got pregnant, and Lew has felt a double loss since his wife died."

"Uh-huh," Betty said. "Well, you go right on believing that if you want to. I know what I'm seeing when he looks at you."

Abby named the baby Jamie Lynn because Lynn was the middle name of Jamie's mother. Lew officially adopted Jamie Lynn, and she took his last name. She was a beautiful baby with bright eyes and traces of red hair.

"It looks like we have another redhead in the family," Betty said. "Boys can't resist a redheaded girl."

Abby had planned to stay off work for two months to take care of the baby, but Lew encouraged her to go to school to get her nursing degree. She couldn't go to school and work at the same time because that would not give her any time to be with the baby. She decided to go to school instead of working. The community college only offered two-year degrees, so she could only get an associate's degree. To be a full RN, she would have to go to a four-year school, but she would address that when the time came.

Abby discovered that she was able go a day or two without thinking of Jamie. She actually dreaded the thought that she might stop altogether. Lew was a good husband.

He didn't give her the same exuberant lust for life that she had when she was with Jamie, but he made her feel safe and secure. Their intimacy was good. He was loving and gentle and gave her what she needed physically.

"You've made me feel like a man again, Abby. I'd forgotten what it feels like to make love to a woman. You're only the second woman I've ever been with. You are just what I needed. You saved my life, Abby. I really do love you."

"I love you too, Lew. You make me feel like a woman again, thank you. And I'm so happy that Jamie Lynn will have you in her life. She will need that as she grows up."

Abby spent the next two years at school. The work load was extensive, but she handled it, often doing her homework late into the night after spending time with Jamie Lynn and putting her to bed. After Abby had completed her associate's degree, the hospital was gracious enough to hire her back, and she was grateful for that because she did so enjoy the work.

Her mother kept Jamie Lynn while Abby worked,

and Jenny enjoyed being a grandmother. By the time the girl was ready for the first grade, she was at an awkward and gangly stage in her life. Bright red hair adorned her head, and her face, while as pretty as was her mother's, contained more freckles, a result of spending a lot of time in the bright Kansas sun.

Abby and Lew had a happy marriage, and both were devoted to their daughter. Lew's reputation as an educator had grown impressively, and he began receiving offers from other colleges and universities around Kansas and even in other states. They were flattering, but he was not inclined to take any of them very seriously because he was reluctant to leave his hometown of Colby, where his ex-wife was buried.

Abby had days when she would pick up a sandwich, drive to the park, and just sit in her car. While eating lunch, she would think about Colorado and Jamie. Sometimes she would start to cry and, often, she could not stop. She occasionally fell into a deep depression that sometimes lasted for days.

She noticed that Lew sometimes seemed to be in the same sort of depression, and, when he was like that, there was nothing she could say or do to help him snap out of it. Eventually, it would let up. She sensed that he might be going through the same trauma that she was experiencing.

One afternoon, she picked up the mail, as she came home from work, and noticed a letter from UCCS—

University of Colorado, Colorado Springs—addressed to Lew. When he came home, she watched him as he read it at the kitchen table.

"Abby," he called to her. "Do you think you would ever want to go back to Colorado?"

Her heart jumped in her chest. "Yes, I think I would someday, maybe," she answered calmly. "Why?"

"I got this offer to teach at the University of Colorado in Colorado Springs. It looks like a pretty good offer, maybe too good an offer to turn down. They want me to come and talk to them. Didn't you live in Colorado Springs?"

"Yes, my dad was stationed at Peterson Air Force Base when he retired. I went to high school there until my senior year."

"You want to ride over there with me for the interview, if your mother can keep Jamie Lynn?"

"Sure, if I can get off work. I can probably change shifts with one of the other girls. When do they want you to come?"

"This coming Thursday," he said.

They left the night before and stayed in a hotel so he could be fresh for the interview.

"Will you make love to me?" she asked him.

"I will," he said, smiling, "I'm sorry, Abby, have I been neglectful of you?"

"Perhaps, I'm too needy?" she said. "You still want me, don't you?"

"No, you're not too needy, I just get—of course, I still want you, Abby. I'll always want you."

"You're a good husband, Lew. I'm glad we met."

"I'm glad too, Abby. Sometimes I think there's a wedge between us, but I went into this marriage with my eyes open. I love you, I love everything about you. Sometimes I wish that there had never been a Peggy and a Jamie and that I had met you first and had fallen in love with you first. But you've been as good a wife as Peggy was."

"But I'm not Peggy."

"I don't mean it like that. You have to know that I'm crazy about you. You make me feel every bit as much of a man as she did."

"I know you are. And you make me happy, Lew, you really do. I hope this position at UCCS is something you really want to do. Whatever you decide, I will be okay with it."

She waited in the lobby while he went in to the interview. He was there about an hour, and, when he came out, he was smiling at her.

"Tell me about it," she insisted.

"I told them I'd let them know in a week, but it's too good a deal to pass up. Will you be okay with moving back here?"

"If that's what you decide is best for us, Lew, then let's do it."

They made the move to Colorado Springs in August

of 1993, in order to be in town for the start of the first semester in September. They also had to get Jamie Lynn registered in school.

They rented a house, with an option to buy, on Westmoreland Road for the first year. Lew would make enough money to support them, so he wanted Abby to stay home and take care of Jamie Lynn. He liked the idea of her not working. She relented, although she had really enjoyed her nursing job in Colby. But it would give her time to spend with her daughter. Unfortunately, she found, it would also give her time to reminisce and remember the past.

໐ຈຄ

After he was released from the hospital, Jamie worked out of the Denver sector and continued to live at home until 1988 when he decided to rent an apartment in Lakewood.

"I'm going to have you partner with another ranger for a few months, Jamie," the chief had told him. "And I may give you some gate-duty, you know, checking cars for proper payment stickers. I know that's no fun for a mountain man like yourself, son, but I just don't want anything to happen to you again."

"I understand, Chief," Jamie told him. "I'm just glad to be back at work."

Usually, he was on fire-watch which was more excit-

ing than taking payment from visitors to the park, but not
by much.

When he moved his belongings out of his room at
the Cain home, he took the pictures of Abby with him.
When his dad brought him some mail, he'd received from
work, to his apartment, he reported back to Jamie's
mother that the pictures were on the wall in Jamie's
apartment bedroom.

In the summer of 1989, Jamie was assigned to go to
The Springs to assist in fire patrol and watch. They had
incurred a number of unexplained and errant campfires.
None had gotten out of control yet, but the concern was
that it could happen. Jamie called his folks and let them
know he would be out of town for a week or so in The
Springs.

"I like The Springs," Jamie explained to his partner,
Landon Smith, one of the rangers who had found him in
the White River Forest. I used to come here when I was a
kid, with my sister and our parents. We drove up Pikes
Peak and went to the Garden of the Gods several times."

But he'd been thinking a lot about it lately, and he
didn't know why. There was nothing special about the
town. It was a much prettier city than Denver, being set
right against the mountains as it was. At least that was his
opinion. Others might differ. He guessed it all depended
on what one was used to.

Lately, he'd been having strange dreams. He'd been
dreaming of a girl almost every night. It was the same girl

every time, but he couldn't make out her face. It was like she was a blur, kind of fading in and fading out. He'd dreamed of girls before, when he was a kid of fifteen years old and older, but that was different. Those girls were always naked, and they were always in the bed in his room. Back then, he'd wake up with a boner. These days he woke up with a terrible feeling of loneliness deep inside.

This girl was trying to wake him up, but he couldn't wake up. He was afraid if he woke up, he would lose her. In his dreams, he rubbed his eyes, trying to clear them so he could see her, see who she was. But he could never see her clearly. They were always in a fog on grassy hills. She was walking, and he was running, but he couldn't catch her. It was always very warm, although the mountains in the distance were snow-capped. He woke up every time, thinking about the girl and trying to remember the dreams. They had become more and more frequent in the past few weeks.

There was precious little time to indulge his mental fabrications, however. He had a job to do and, given his accident and prolonged recovery, he certainly could not afford to suffer any let up in the performance of that job. He joined his assigned team and set out on his fire-watch patrol.

He was working again with Landon Smith when they were asked to check out reports that some people were poaching deer out of season in the Pike National Forest north of the old ghost town of Tarryall in Park County.

"Tarryall?" Landon said, "where the hell is that?"

"Beats Me," Jamie replied. "That's why we have maps." He stretched out the map on the hood of their truck and began looking for their destination. He found the name, Tarryall, in the index and then wrote down the directions.

"Woodland Park, then stay on Twenty-Four through Divide, Florissant, and Lake George. Just past Lake George, turn right on Tarryall Road and drive into the Pike National Forest and see what we can see."

When they arrived at Tarryall, they discovered that, although it was abandoned, there appeared to be evidence that someone had either been staying in the area or visiting there on a regular basis.

"I bet this place is jumping on Saturday night," Landon said.

"You going to bring a date here sometime?"

"Looks like it gets pretty dark here at night. I think I'll pass on that."

They drove on through the abandoned community for a few miles until they heard some rifle fire from the trees in the foothills.

Jamie pulled the truck over and parked it. "Okay, we'll take side-arms and rifles, come on." They exited the vehicle, armed themselves, and started walking toward the sound of the last gunshot they heard. They crept through the trees until they could hear men's voices.

They couldn't make out what was being said, mainly laughing and some cursing.

Creeping a little closer, they could see four men field dressing several deer they had shot. Jamie spoke almost in a whisper to Landon. "I want you to sneak around to the right through that little stand of trees over there." He pointed in that direction.

"Right," Landon said. "I see it."

"I'm going to go in behind them over on this other side to back you up. You'll be able to see me. You'll make the initial confrontation. Just step out of the trees with your rifle pointed at them. Order them to move away from their weapons. Make them move back toward me. I'll gauge their demeanor and watch them to see if they are complying with your order, or if they get any crazy ideas, okay?"

"Got it," Landon said.

"Be aggressive," Jamie said. "Don't give them a chance to think about challenging you."

"Okay," Landon said, nodding his head.

It took Landon two minutes to get in place and Jamie less time than that to get behind the four men. He was less than twenty feet from them, and they did not suspect that he was there. At this point, the rangers had the tactical advantage.

Jamie caught Landon's eye and gave him a thumbs-up. Landon immediately stepped out of the trees and shouted at the men, as he walked quickly toward them with his rifle raised. "Step back," he shouted. "Step back away from the deer and don't reach for your rifles. Keep your hands out of your pockets and move back, *now!*"

The men recoiled in shock, but they did as they were told, albeit somewhat reluctantly.

Landon drew to within twenty feet of them and kept his rifle trained on them. "Don't anybody move," he yelled. He could tell they were trying to assess the situation and their chances of getting out of this without going to jail. He guessed they were thinking that there was only one ranger, and there were four of them.

From where Jamie was standing, he could see everything the men were doing. They were anxious, that was obvious, and definitely worried about the possibility of their ending up in jail. The man in the rear, closest to Jamie, had a pistol in his rear pocket, a pistol that Landon couldn't see. The man's right hand was inching slowly toward the weapon as he apparently weighed in his mind the advantages and disadvantages of drawing the weapon and using it to get them out of their current predicament.

As he reached for the pistol, apparently having made the decision to use it, he heard a calm but very stern voice from behind him.

"If you pull that pistol, I'll send you to hell," Jamie said. He walked toward the group with his rifle raised and pointed at them. The man froze in place and put his hands in the air.

Jamie raised his voice. "On the ground, all of you.

Get on the ground and put your hands behind your backs. You're under arrest for poaching deer. And if 'you' give me any shit—" He pointed at the man who started to draw the gun from his pocket. "—I'll charge you with attempted murder of a National Park Ranger."

"You can't do that," the man said.

"Maybe not," Jamie said, "but think about this. I *could* have waited until you drew the gun out of your pocket and shot you dead, but I didn't, so consider this your lucky day. You'll be going to jail and not into the ground."

The man turned pale as he considered that possibility.

They dropped the men off at the sheriff's office in Woodland Park and headed back to The Springs.

"You did a hell of a job back there, Landon," Jamie told him. "Your elevated level of aggression took them by surprise and stopped them from challenging you. You saved the day."

"You're blowing smoke up my ass, Jamie, but I appreciate it. Your plan worked out right. If we had gone charging in there together, that fella might have pulled that gun and shot one of us, or both of us before we could have reacted."

"I know, that's why I wanted to get behind them. But I was serious. If you hadn't been as forceful as you were, they might not have backed off away from their rifles, and we could have had an OK Corral right there."

"I see what you mean," Landon acknowledged.

Heavy rains began in the high country a couple of days before Jamie was scheduled to return to Denver. The immediate wildfire threat was alleviated for a while, so he was able to leave early. He decided to spend few hours in Manitou Springs. His folks had taken him and his sister there once, on one of their trips to Pikes Peak, and he found the little town quaint and interesting. There was an arts and crafts fair going on, and he bought a couple of things for his mother and sister.

He also came across a studio that featured music, poetry, and painting objects. He'd never had much interest in poetry, but he found a poem entitled "In Dreams" which kind of reminded him of the dreams he'd been having lately. He bought a frame with a glass to put it in and decided he would hang it on the wall in his apartment.

He drove a nail into the wall next to the picture of the girl he had brought from his room at home. When he set the poem on the nail, and carefully straightened it, he glanced over at the picture of the girl. He stared at the picture for a moment and then went to the telephone and called his mother.

After two rings, his mother answered. "Hello."

"Hi, Mom," Jamie said.

"Hello, darling," his mother replied. "How are you doing?"

"I don't know," he said

"Oh, okay, well, just tell me what you've got on your mind."

"Mom, who is the girl in the picture on my wall?"

This was the moment his mother had been dreading since her son had come back home. She had no idea what to tell him.

"Son, your dad and I are going to have to come and sit down with you an explain some things to you. It's not something I can talk to you about over the phone."

"Just tell me her name, Mom. I need to know her name. I've been dreaming about her for a month or so now. I need to know who she is."

"Are you sure you don't want to come home and talk with me and Dad about it?" she asked him.

"I just need to know her name, Mom."

"Her name is Abby, Jamie."

"Okay, Mom, thank you." He told her and hung up the phone.

"Oh, my God, what have I done?" his mother said to herself out loud. She immediately called her husband at his office and told him what had happened.

"I'll check on him," Will said.

೭⁄೨೭⁄೨

Jamie opened the door of his apartment and found his dad standing there. "Hey, Dad," he said. "What's going on?"

"Your mother called me and said she told you about the picture of Abby."

"I need to find out where she is, Dad."

"Jamie, we don't know where she is. She was torn apart by your disappearance. She came to the house a couple of times and was in a pretty bad way. Your mother was worried about her. She took your loss very hard. Her father passed away not long after you were lost."

"Oh, damn! I didn't know that," Jamie said.

"That hit Abby pretty hard too, but losing you devastated her. Honestly, we all thought you were dead. Abby thought you were dead. She didn't seem to be in her right mind. After not hearing from her for quite some time, your mother went to their house in Golden, and they were gone. They had moved and left no forwarding address. I'm sorry, son. We just don't know where she is." His father studied him a moment. "You took her picture with you when you left our house, but you haven't asked about her until now. Why is that, son?"

"I don't know, Dad. I think my mind blocked her out, and I never really noticed her before now. I think I took the photo instinctively when I left home without realizing I was even doing it."

"I think you're right, son. Maybe you weren't ready to deal with this before now." His father shrugged. "But we don't even know for certain that she's still alive. I pray she is, but we just don't know."

"She's alive, Dad. I know that."

"How can you know that, Jamie?"

"She's been coming to me in my dreams."

Chapter 5

Searching

Jamie was rummaging through the boxes of his belongings his mother had packed for him and he found a photo album he'd had. It was one of those fold out kind with multiple windows into which pictures were inserted. There were fifty or so pictures of hunting trips and campsites and such. One or two shots showed him standing by a tree with a deer he'd apparently brought down. And in another similar picture he was standing beside a man he recognized as his brother-in-law, Evan Garner.

Most of the pictures, however, were of Abby in different poses, mugging for the camera, smiling, laughing at him or ignoring him. There were a few of the two of them, that someone else had taken, in which he was carrying her or she was on his shoulders. In one picture, she was sitting on the bed in a bedroom and had his ranger hat on and not much else. He stared at that one for quite a long time.

It was like looking at two other people who were apparently very happy at one time in their lives. He recognized himself in the picture with the beautiful girl but he could barely remember ever having been involved with her in the events displayed in the photographs.

The dreams did not stop. The girl didn't come every night but she still came to him at random times. It was like she only came when she could find the time to come. He eventually remembered enough to know that he had been in love with Abby, and he suspected he still was. He knew he had to find her. He took the poem out of its frame and, with a marker, wrote her name across the top just under the title.

He couldn't remember exactly where Abby's house was in Golden, but he thought he might recognize it if he drove around in the general area where she and her family had lived. He had to wait until the weekend because he couldn't do personal business when he was working and was in a company truck.

It took three weekends of random driving up and down the streets before he recognized the house where the Prentiss family had lived. He stopped and went up to the door and knocked. A man came to the door.

"Hello, sir," Jamie said. "I'm sorry to bother you, but I'm looking for someone who used to live in this house. Did you, by any chance, know the people who lived here before you?"

"Well, I've been here almost two years, young man," the man said. "I didn't know them but I can direct you to the owner of the property, he might be able to help you."

"I'd certainly appreciate that, sir, thank you."

The man left for a moment and returned with a business card. "This is the guy," he said and handed Jamie the card.

"Many thanks," Jamie said.

"No problem," the man replied.

∾∾∾

"Mark Prentiss was the best renter I ever had," Dave Neely told Jamie. "He always paid his rent on time and kept the yard mowed. He even did a lot of the upkeep on the house that most renters usually complain to me about. When he died, the mother was a wreck. She gave me a month's notice that they were leaving and asked for their deposit back. Hell, yeah, I gave it back to her. The daughter had lost her fiancé, they said. He was lost in the mountains or something, and they never found him. She was really torn up about that. Beautiful girl but she looked like she was about to lose her mind. I felt just awful for them both. They didn't tell me where they were going, and I didn't want to bother them about it. Are you related to them somehow?"

"I'm the fiancé who was missing," Jamie said.

"Oh, holy shit," Neely said. "I read about you, you're the park ranger that was missing for so long?"

"Yes, sir."

"Oh, damn, man. I wish I could be more help to you, but I just don't know any more than what I told you."

"Well, thank you, Mr. Neely, I appreciate it," Jamie told, him and went back to his truck.

That night, the girl returned to him in his dreams. He felt the warm air blowing across his face, and the fog rolled in as he walked barefoot over cool grass toward the shadowy female figure. The figure seemed to be floating just above the ground before her feet touched it. She was walking forward but looking back at him, and, this time, he could see her face. It was Abby, and suddenly she was standing by her locker in the hall of Golden High School. She was talking to him and about to walk away when he stopped her.

In his dream, he saw their life together again, when they met at their lockers in the hall. They were having burgers, fries, and cokes after school. He saw when he first told her he loved her, on top of Lookout Mountain, and the first time they made love in his room, at his house in Coal Creek Canyon. He saw everything they had done for the two years they knew each other until he drove away that day, heading for an unforeseen destiny that would separate them for God only knows how long.

He would find her. He had to find her, no matter how long it took. He realized he still loved her, and he would never stop loving her. The dreams would not stop until he found her. They would keep her close to him, and they would keep him close to her until that day she returned to him.

Jamie was hopeful that, since Abby's family had moved to Golden from The Springs, she might have returned to that area. He checked phone books but found no Abby, or Jenny, Prentiss.

He didn't know of any other relatives of the Prentiss family. He didn't even know where Abby's dad was from originally.

He used the park services' system to check driver's licenses and found no driver's license in Abby's name. He wondered if perhaps she had gotten married. How could he possibly know what her married name would be now? He ran an ad in the personals, *Seeking information on Abby Prentiss. Contact Jamie Cain.* And he included his phone number. He ran the ad for a year but never received a response.

He battled recurring bouts of depression as month after month turned into year after year with no success.

In 1995, the chief asked Jamie to come to his office for a meeting. Jamie showed up, and the chief met him in the lobby. "Come on in, Jamie," he said.

"What's up, boss?" Jamie asked.

"Jamie, the service needs you to relocate to the Pueblo sector, if it won't be too much of a hardship on you. They are seriously undermanned and, frankly, they need the help. Can you do it?"

"I guess I can. It's not my favorite part of the world, but I'll go where the job needs me, I suppose."

"Good. I'll be beholden to you. I promised them I'd send them a good guy. We'll cover your moving expenses and the lease on your apartment, and you'll get a couple of weeks per diem."

Jamie called his mother, who was not pleased with the news.

"They hung in there with me during my troubles, and the least I can do is go where I'm needed," he told his parents.

Eventually, Jamie bought a cabin about twenty-five miles out of Pueblo in Beulah Valley near the small town of Beulah. The cabin was located on Highway 78 and sat off the road a short distance up, on a rise. It provided an excellent view of the surrounding countryside from the covered deck. It had an unfinished basement where the propane fired furnace and the washer and dryer were located. A fireplace, which he loved to keep roaring in the winter, kept the place too warm, more often than not. The cabin would have been a very lonely place had Jamie been a social animal, but he inherently was not.

One Friday night, Jamie was in a nightspot in Pueblo. His intention had been to have a couple of beers and listen to the music for a while. He perceived that he had caught the interest of two women at a table just a few feet away from his. They were both attractive, but the little blonde looked as if she took better care of herself. Her friend was already on her way to being too drunk to be very interesting.

Jamie pointed at the blonde-haired woman and made a circle with his index finger, indicating that he wanted to dance. She smiled and nodded her head, so he stood up and walked toward the dance floor and she met him there.

"I'm Kelly," she said as he took her in his arms and they started to slow dance.

"Hello, Kelly," Jamie said. "I'm happy to meet you. My name is Jamie."

"What do you do, good looking?"

"I work for the National Park Service," Jamie told her.

"You're a park ranger?"

"Yes, I am."

She was dressed sexy, but not trashy. Her dress revealed enough cleavage that he could see her breasts, and she had nothing to be ashamed of. She was a pretty woman, he guessed about twenty-four years of age. Her hair came down just over her ears and flipped out at the edges. It looked natural, but he couldn't tell for sure.

"What do you do, Kelly?"

"I'm a dental hygienist," she said.

"So, you spend a lot of time in people's mouths?"

"More than my share," she said, chuckling.

"Your friend looks like she's had about enough, don't you think?" Jamie said.

"Becky? Yeah, Becky always drinks too much. She's here with some other friends so she won't have to drive home drunk."

"That's good," he said. "So, you can come sit at my table and talk to me a while?"

"I can if you want me too, Jamie."

"I'd like that."

She picked up her purse, moved over to his table, and sat down next to him. They danced again, and then he ordered them a couple more drinks.

"Where do you live?" she asked him.

"I have a cabin out on Seventy-Eight near Beulah. Do you know where that is?"

"I've heard of it," she said, "but I've never been there. I bet it's pretty out that way, isn't it?"

"It's beautiful," he replied.

"I'd like to see it sometime," she said.

"You want to see it in the morning?"

She smiled and nodded her head like a teenager.

⁂

She undressed in front of him, in his bedroom, and he kissed her passionately for several minutes until it felt as if she was getting weak.

He picked her up and carried her to the bed, laid her down, and pulled back the covers. She got under the covers as he undressed.

It didn't come to his mind how long it had been since he was with Abby. It had been nine years, but just being in bed with a woman, any woman, would never fill the void that losing Abby had left in him. In the dark of his room, this night, with this woman, this beautiful woman, in his mind, he was again with Abby. He lost himself in her. It was only by the strictest of discipline and control that he didn't call her Abby. They made love again later that night, and it was no less passionately than the first time.

It was not until he woke up the next morning, and saw Kelly lying beside him, that he snapped out of his fantasy. She reached across the bed and caressed his arm. He kissed her. "You're beautiful, Kelly," he told her.

"My God, Jamie," she said, "No man has ever made me feel like that before."

"It was good for me too, Kelly," he said. "You want some breakfast."

"Sure, if you don't mind."

"Not a bit. I'll make us some coffee first. We can eat on the deck."

"This is a beautiful cabin, Jamie, but it must get lonely if you live here alone."

"I'm on the road a lot," he said.

As Jamie made breakfast, Kelly was wandering

around the cabin, drinking her coffee, just admiring his décor and looking out the windows at the mountains. She saw the poem on the wall and read it. She didn't ask about the girl's name he'd written on the top of the page. It was self-explanatory.

"Will you call me if I give you my number? I'd like to see you again if you feel the same way."

"Sure, Kelly, I'd like to see you again sometime." He took down her number and gave her his.

৩৵৵৩

Most nights when he was at home, he would sit on his deck drinking coffee and brooding, thinking of all the things he might have done to change the circumstances that had ruined his life. But it was all to no avail. He couldn't change the past. How could he have known that last trip he made to Grand Junction with Abby would be the last time he would ever see her again?

What was he missing? he kept asking himself. He had searched for Abby everywhere he knew to search. But where had she been before she had come into his life? Of course, it came to him in a moment, Colorado Springs. Abby went to school in The Springs.

How stupid of him that he'd never asked her where she went to high school in The Springs. He found that it would be a laborious and time-consuming effort to check out every high school in The Springs.

He called The Springs School District and was told that there were almost thirty high schools in the Colorado Springs metropolitan area.

He couldn't use his company cell phone to call every one of them because it would run up too many minutes, and he was supposed to be discretionary about personal use of company property. His solution was to get his own private cell phone.

This approach immediately taught him that the school administrations would not reveal any information to him over the phone. He would either have to visit each and every school or write letters to them and hope they would respond.

Getting around to every school in The Springs could take him a year unless he waited until his vacation came up. Then he could probably do it in that two-week period.

There was a new thing out now, just developed in the last couple of years. It was called email. Email required a computer and other stuff he knew absolutely nothing about, and not everyone had it in their places of business. He was beginning to feel helpless and that he was fighting a losing battle. But, while in the office one afternoon, he noticed one of the office staff, a lady named Joan, working on a computer.

"Joan," he asked, "can you send email on that computer?

"Sure, Jamie, it's easy," Joan said. "Do you want to send a letter to someone?"

"No, I'm trying to locate someone who went to high school in Colorado Springs in eighty-two and eighty-three. The problem is I don't know which school."

"Holy crud," Joan replied. "That's quite an assignment. First, we'll need to know which schools have been built since then, that shouldn't be too hard. Then we have to know which schools have email available. Most schools have fax machines available these days so we could go that route, too, if they don't have email."

Jamie nodded. "I'll get you the list of schools and whether they have email or not. What else will you need?"

"Get their email addresses and their fax numbers. Write a letter telling me the info you need, and I'll send it out for you."

"It'll take me a little while to get all that together, but when I do, I'll bring you the list."

"I'll do my best." Joan said."

"Thanks, Joan, I appreciate the help."

He began to imagine what he would say to Abby once he found her. He had to consider the possibility that she had gotten married. What if she had gotten married and had a houseful of kids by now? It had been almost ten years. He couldn't expect a girl, a woman, like Abby to not meet someone and get married and have kids. What in the world did he think he was doing? He called his mother.

"Mom, what if I find Abby, and she's married and has children?"

"Well, son, if you ever find out where she is, you need to try and find out what her marital status is before you go and see her. You do understand why, don't you?"

"Yes, Mom, I know I can't just walk up to her house and knock on the door, not knowing who is going to answer. She has a life of her own by now, and that life may include another man and his children."

"You have to be prepared for that, Jamie. I know that's hard to contemplate, but it's reality."

"I'd rather that be the case, Mom, than to find out she's dead."

"I know, and I pray that Abby is still alive."

"I'm going to come home for a few days. I need to get back to basics for a while."

"Oh, that would be wonderful, Jamie. Your dad and I would love to see you."

He arranged for a few days off and made the drive north to Coal Creek Canyon.

"Why did this happen to me, Dad?" he asked, as he and his folks sat on the back patio, watching the sun going down over the front range.

"There are things that happen in life, Jamie, that there are just no logical explanations for. One day your life is clicking along perfectly, and, in a heartbeat, it goes to hell. It can change just that quickly.

A week before I was scheduled to muster out of the

navy, my crew flew into a storm, five-hundred miles from land out in the Atlantic. We lost both engines and were forced to ditch. We were adrift for a day and a half before we were rescued. Now, I was lucky, but your mother was a wreck when I got back, but we got through it okay. The point is that it could have changed everything that has happened to us since that time. Your sister would never have known me. Your mother would have eventually married someone else and would probably still be living in Maine now. And you would be somebody else's son."

"I wouldn't like that, Pop."

"Neither would I," Will said

Jamie laughed. "But I have to find her, I have to find Abby, even if I find her and she's married and has a houseful of kids. I have to know that she's okay."

"I understand that, I really do, and I agree with it. I think you should find her. You have to put your mind at ease."

Jamie stayed a couple of days at home and then headed back to Beulah Valley. The next morning was Sunday. A knock on his door woke him up early. He opened the door to find Kelly standing there.

"Well, hello," he said. "You want some coffee?"

"I was worried about you," she said. "I've been calling, but you didn't return my calls."

"I went to see my parents for a few days," he told her. "They live in the mountains, and cell phones don't work up there very well, so I usually turn mine off when I get off the freeways in the high country. Are you okay?"

"I just wanted to see you," she said.

"Let's go sit on the deck. I'll bring the coffee." When he brought their coffee and some cream and sugar for her, he sat down.

"I'm glad you came, Kelly. I really enjoyed being with you the other night."

"Will you make love to me again, Jamie?

"Kelly, you were wonderful, but there's something I have to tell you."

"I know you have someone else. I saw the poem on your wall and the girl's name on it."

"I don't really want to talk about that, Kelly. I can't," he said.

"But you made me feel like no man has ever made me feel. I can help you, Jamie. I can help you get over her."

"I don't want to get over her, Kelly," he said.

"I don't understand," she said. "You loved me like you were in love with me. I believed you were in love with me. You were gentle and loving. You were perfect, everything a woman wants in a man. I fell for you head over heels just after that one night. I felt like we were made for each other."

"I'm sorry, Kelly, I'm really sorry. I didn't mean to mislead you. You're a good lover. It wasn't all my doing. You made me feel like no woman has made me feel in a very long time. Abby is the girl I was going to marry. Circumstances beyond our control prevented that, and I lost contact with her. I don't know where she is, and I'm still searching for her. The only way I can make love to another woman is to pretend she's Abby."

"Oh my God, Jamie, you're telling me that you threw a mad loving on me, and all the time you were pretending I was someone else?"

"I know it was inconsiderate and selfish, Kelly, but I'm a man with normal physical needs like any man, and you're a beautiful, desirable woman. The truth is that I wanted you, badly. I wanted to go to bed with you, but when it came down to it, I couldn't do it without thinking of Abby. I'm sorry."

"Well, it's not like you forced me into it. It was wonderful, and I wish it could continue, but I guess I'll have to look at it like it was a surrealistic threesome that I really enjoyed. I hope you find that girl, Jamie. You need her more than you need me. I'm not going to call you anymore. This is pain that I can't afford, so I'm going to stop it before it goes any further."

"Listen, Kelly, I could continue with you, but it wouldn't be fair to you. I'm never going to love another woman. If I told you I might love you some day, just to sleep with you, it would be a lie, and it would be wrong. I'm going to have a lot of lonely nights ahead of me, lying in my bed, wishing I'd lied to you."

She chuckled.

"So, it's good that we're having this conversation when I'm not horny," he said.

"Oh, God, what a waste," she said. "I wish it could be different, Jamie."

"I do too, Kelly, I really do," he said.

She left, and he wondered if he had made a mistake. Kelly had been a "port in a storm," so to speak. He could make a good case for keeping her around, but it would require dishonesty of the highest caliber. He didn't want to go there.

Jamie began to compile a list of every high school in the Colorado Springs metropolitan area. Phone calls made over a two-month period eventually produced a record of email addresses and/or fax numbers. He gave the list to Joan at the station, along with Abby's full name and the years she attended school in The Springs. In about a week, Joan had one positive response back.

She called Jamie. "Abby went to Mitchell High School. It's near Peterson Air Force Base," she told him. "They say she transferred to Golden High School in 'eight-four, but you already knew that, didn't you, Jamie?"

"Yeah, that's where I met her. Okay, Joan, thank you, I appreciate the help. Aw, crap," he said to himself. He should have foreseen that. He was chasing rainbows. And he should have known the Prentiss family would have been living near the base and that Abby would go to schools near the base. He could have saved some time by checking that area first. Well, it was done now.

It was just a feeling, perhaps wishful hoping or delusion on his part, but he believed that Abby was in The Springs. He didn't know why he felt that way, just a feeling, but he felt her presence every time he went through the town. Sometimes, he just drove randomly through the streets just to sense her presence, hoping he might catch a glimpse of her.

His only comfort came from watching the sun go down over the mountains in the evening as he sat drinking coffee on his deck. God, how he wished he knew where she was. He'd never been a religious man. It would be hypocrisy for him to start praying now, but he had nowhere else to turn. If Abby was still alive, he hoped God was watching over her, keeping her happy and safe. And he hoped she thought about him sometimes.

Chapter 6

Separate Ways

Jamie Lynn began the second grade in 1993 at an elementary school near their house on Westmoreland Road. At seven-years-old, she was still a gangly sort of girl, but her face was changing. She was beginning to look more and more like her mother every day. And her previously obtrusive freckles were beginning to disappear, except for a very lightly colored line of them across her nose. She had her mother's hair and eyes. She was an embodiment of the old cliché, "She is her mother's daughter."

The highlight of Jamie Lynn's after -school day was the arrival home of her daddy, Lew. If any man was ever meant to be a father, it was Lew Morgan. He practically worshipped his bright-eyed "garden fairy" of a step-daughter, as he referred to her.

"Come play with me, Daddy," she'd call to him, just like she did when she first started talking. He would stop whatever he was doing, go sit down on the floor, and play blocks or dolls or have a tea party with her.

"I need more tea, Jamie Lynn," he told her, holding up his cup.

"It's not ready yet, Daddy."

"Oh, well excuse me, miss. Just pour me another cup when it's ready, if you don't mind."

"Can we play something else now?" she would often say."

"What would you like to play, sweetheart?"

She would run to her room and return with any one of a number of games. No matter how tired or busy he might be, Lew would play with her until her mother's pre-set time for her to do her homework.

"She's going to look just like you, Abby," Lew said, one night. "How did your dad keep the boys respectful around you, without shooting a few of them?"

Abby laughed. "My dad was a very imposing man. He wasn't an inherently mean man but he 'looked' mean. I mean, he looked like Charles Bronson, and nobody would mess with him. I had a few boyfriends in high school, and the smart ones became friends with my dad right away."

"I wish I could have known him," Lew said. "My guess is he was a quiet man."

"He was, and why do you guess that, because my mother talks so much?"

Lew smiled.

"I knew it," Abby said.

"She is quite a talker," he replied.

"Dad pretty much ignored her because she babbled all the time, and that just made her babble all that much more."

"I hope we never get like that, Abby," he said.

"You're a quiet man, Lew, but I bet you'll be very protective of Jamie Lynn when she starts going out with boys."

"Well, let's see. I'm thirty-three. When she starts dating at twenty-five—"

"Twenty-five!" Jamie Lynn interjected loudly. "Daddy!"

"I'll be fifty-years-old, so I might ought to take some boxing lessons or something. Of course, my preference would be that she wait until she's married before she starts dating."

The girl glanced at her mother with a bewildered look on her face and mouthed, "Mom?"

"He's playing, darling," Abby said. "You know how Daddy likes to tease you."

"When can I start dating, Daddy?"

"You're eight years old, honey, don't you think it's a

little early to be thinking about dating at your age?"

"When do kids start dating?" she asked them.

"I'm going to defer to your mother on that," Lew said."

"Oh, thanks," Abby said, frowning at him." "Well, Jamie Lynn, most young girls start dating around fifteen or so. And that is usually with a chaperone or monitored by parents in some way. I prefer that, when you start dating, it will be on double dates."

What does chaperone mean?"

"It means a parent goes along with you. Like if you went to a movie with a boy and Daddy went along and sat in a seat right behind you."

"How old would I have to be to do that?"

"I don't know. Why are you asking this? Did a boy ask you out on a date?"

"Mm-huh, Tommy Baker asked me to go to a movie with him. He said his mother would take us."

"Is Tommy in your class?"

"No, he's in the fourth-grade. He's nine."

Abby looked at Lew, who was shaking his head. "Daddy and I will talk about this, honey. I'll have to meet his mother first. I'm not saying no, but I'm not saying yes either. We'll talk about it and see."

⁂

Abby was driving along Interstate 25, after dropping

off some paperwork that Lew had inadvertently left at home, when a National Park Services truck drew alongside her. Because traffic was rather congested, the truck stayed next to her for a mile or so. She wanted to look over to see who was driving the truck, but she was reluctant to take her eyes off the road. She imagined the driver was looking over at her. She eventually risked a glance over at the truck, but the widows were tinted, and she couldn't get a good look at the driver. It was a man, she was certain, but what was she expecting? Did she think she would see Jamie driving the truck? And what if he had been, what would she do then? What could she do?

Abby had never considered what she would do if she suddenly discovered that, by some miracle, Jamie was still alive. Suppose he walked back into her life one day, with that happy-go-lucky manner of his, and said, "Where you been, baby? I've been looking for you for ten years. I still love you." What would she do? Would she leave Lew and go back to the love of her life? She didn't honestly know.

She picked up Jamie Lynn from school and took her home. When the girl was busy doing her homework, Abby went out to the gazebo in the backyard, buried her face in her hands, and wept like her world had come apart. She didn't hear Lew come home from work and put his car in the garage. Nor did she see him standing at the rear sliding door watching her crying her heart out in the gazebo.

೮/೨೮/೨

In 1996, Jamie Lynn was ten-years-old, and Lew was sufficiently comfortable with allowing her to go to a movie with Tommy Baker. Tommy, who had taken a shine to the delightful little red-headed girl in the fourth grade, was still enamored with her as they both had aged and grown.

Jamie Lynn was looking more and more like her mother with each passing day. Tommy was slightly taller than the girl but heavier. He was a good-looking boy, not what one would call handsome, but good looking and loaded with personality. The two mothers, Abby and Vera Baker, had to admit that the kids did make a cute couple. They both chaperoned them to the movies on occasion, and Abby and Lew took them on outings to the mountains every so often.

"Where are we going today, Mr. Morgan?" Tommy asked.

"How does Cheyenne Canyon sound, Tommy?"

"Great," he replied.

"Have you been there before?"

"No, sir," Tommy said.

"It's great," Jamie Lynn told him. "You'll like it, we go there all the time."

The two kids sat in the back seat of Lew's car, and Tommy spoke the name aloud as they entered the canyon. "North Cheyenne Canon."

"It's Canyon, Tommy, that's the Spanish spelling of Canyon," Jamie Lynn said. Tommy nodded.

"We're going to Helen Hunt Falls," Lew said. "It's just up ahead a short ways."

Lew parked the car, and they got out. "Come on," he said, "let's go up the stairs. We're going to hike up the trail above the falls."

The two "women" forged on ahead while Lew and Tommy lagged behind.

"Hey, the women are getting ahead of us," Lew said. "We can't let that happen. Come on Tommy, let's catch up and get in front."

"Yeah!" Tommy shouted.

They started running up the hill, caught up to, and ran around them. Abby and Jamie Lynn just watched them run for about fifty feet more and then stop to catch their breath. Mother and daughter walked calmly by as the two guys were still trying to recover from the uphill sprint.

"You look a little out of shape, Tommy," Lew said."

"Me? What about you, Mr. Morgan?"

"I'm a professor, Tommy. Besides, I'm thirty-five-years-old."

"Oh yeah, make excuses," the boy shot back.

Lew started laughing. "That was a pretty good comeback, Tommy," he said and ruffled the boy's hair. "I'm going to start jogging and take you on again."

Tommy was beaming and obviously enjoying the attention he was receiving from Jamie Lynn's dad.

"Where does everyone want to go for lunch," Lew asked them after they were back at the visitor center.

"Red Top," Jamie Lynn shouted.

"Red Top? Is that okay with everyone? Do you like Red Top Burgers, Tommy?"

"I don't know," he said. "I've never been there."

"Best burgers in town," Lew said

"Best burgers in the world," Jamie Lynn corrected him.

"Now, how would you know that, darling,? Where else in the world have you had burgers?"

"Kansas," she replied.

"Okay, fair point," Lew said. "That's the only world you've known so far. So Red Top it is."

When they dropped Tommy off at his house, Abby and Lew took the opportunity to meet the Bakers. Abby already knew Vera Baker, Tommy's mother, from school and had gone with her to the movies with their kids, but neither she nor Lew had met Tommy's father.

Mark Baker was a gruff looking man who had the physical appearance of an alcoholic, or more accurately, a drunk. He was congenial enough, but his breath reeked of booze, and Lew noticed that Baker made an overly appreciative assessment of Abby's physical attributes. The mother looked as if she might have been attractive, perhaps ten years ago, but life seemed to have caught up with her.

Tommy was noticeably embarrassed by his parents.

"You want to come in and have a beer?" Mark asked them.

"No thank you, maybe some other time," Lew replied. "We need to get on home."

"Okay, well thanks for taking the boy with you today."

"No problem," Lew said, "Tommy's a great kid."

"That's a lovely couple," Lew said, as they drove away from the Baker's house.

"Now, let's try not to judge them just by their appearance after only one visit," Abby said.

"Let's talk about this after we get Jamie Lynn home."

"Tommy is my boyfriend," Jamie Lynn said from the back seat.

"I know, honey, and Tommy is a good kid, but your mother and I have to be careful about what kinds of people you get mixed up with."

"But Tommy is not like his dad," she replied.

"Daddy isn't saying you can't be friends with Tommy, Jamie Lynn," Abby said. "He's just saying we have to be careful."

"I don't know what that means," Jamie Lynn said.

"I tell you what we'll do," Lew said. "We'll invite them over for dinner one night and get to know them a little better. How's that sound?"

"Okay, Daddy, that sounds good."

Later, Lew and Abby were sitting on the back patio, drinking coffee. There was silence between them for quite some time until Lew finally spoke.

"I came in early from work last week and saw you sitting in the gazebo, crying."

Abby looked stunned, not knowing how to respond but having no intention of lying to him. "I'm sorry. Lew, I was having a bout of depression."

"I get that sometimes too," he said. "I wish there were something I could do for you when that happens, Abby. But I can't be him."

Tears came to Abby's eyes. "Oh, Lew, I'm so sorry. It's not that you're not enough. You're a good husband and a wonderful father. My life has been so blessed because of you. You've made life so much better for me and Jamie Lynn. I could never imagine it without you."

"But your heart still aches for Jamie. I know it does. I've seen the look in your eyes when you talk to Jamie Lynn about him and those times when I see you just sitting alone deep in thought. I know because I still have the same thoughts about Peggy from time to time, not as often as I used to have but it still happens."

"I'm really sorry, Lew. I guess if I had gone to his funeral and seen his body and would have known for certain that he was dead, I could put it behind me. But I keep having this heart-wrenching feeling that he might be out there somewhere. I know it's crazy, I know it's not true, but sometimes it makes me almost want to die."

"I want you to do something for me and for you."

"Okay," Abby said. "What is it?"

"I want you to go back to school and finish the work for your nursing degree."

"I'd love to do that, but why now?"

"I just think you need to be able to take care of yourself and Jamie Lynn if something should happen to me. I have a decent life insurance policy, but I'd feel more comfortable if I knew you were self-sufficient. You can go to UCCS. They have some really good nursing programs."

"I'll look into it, Lew, I'd like to do that."

രാരാ

A cookout seemed like a good idea to Lew, as a way to get to know Tommy Baker's mom and dad. After all, their children had been in as serious a "relationship" as two adolescent children could be in. They had been friends for two years. And Tommy's mother had confessed to Abby that Tommy was truly smitten with her daughter.

Abby didn't get too excited about it. The boy was only eleven years old, but he seemed to be a very nice boy.

The Bakers showed up at the Morgans' house with Mark Baker already slightly inebriated and toting a six-pack of beer.

"Come on in guys," Lew told them, "I'll put the steaks on the grill."

Abby led Vera Baker out to the patio, and Tommy and Jamie Lynn followed along with them. The two kids went to the gazebo, sat down, and started talking.

"You want me to put your beer in the fridge, Mark?" Lew said. Mark nodded and handed him the beer, then the two of them went outside and sat down next to the women. Abby poured Lew and Vera some iced tea, and Lew sipped his as he got up and tended to the steaks on the grill.

"You don't drink, Lew?" Mark asked.

"I do on occasion but not usually on family outings. I used to drink some when I was younger, but I gave it up when I got older. My job won't allow me to drink a lot now."

"I don't drink during the week much," Mark replied. "I save it for the weekends."

"I could do that too, I suppose," Lew said, "and we have a glass of wine every so often when Abby fixes Italian food. But when Jamie Lynn came along, I pretty much decided not to drink in front of her to the extent that I might end up drunk in her presence."

"Oh, well I usually just get a buzz. I don't usually get shit-faced, if you know what I mean."

"Yeah, I know," Lew said.

"Now, Mark, you watch your mouth," his wife yelled at him.

"I'm sorry, Vera," he said. Then, being too 'buzzed' to be discreet and just shut up, he stood up and went over to Abby.

"Abby, I've had a little too much to drink, and I'm sorry if I offended you with my language. You're too nice a lady to have to hear that kind of talk, and I'm sorry."

"It's okay, Mark," she said. "I've heard worse. Why don't you go sit at the table, and Lew will have the steaks ready in just a little while?"

"Mark, go sit your ass down and leave her alone," Vera said.

Abby noticed that Tommy was watching his dad's antics from the gazebo. Jamie Lynn was talking to Tommy and appeared not to have seen or heard any of it.

After they had eaten, Abby and Vera were busying themselves cleaning up the dishes and bowls and silverware while Lew and Mark sat on the patio, talking. Mark had indulged in a couple of more beers by that time. Lew couldn't help but notice that his eyes followed Abby everywhere she went. He made no effort to hide his leering, no sneaking a glance here and there but watched her as if her husband was not even there.

"Mark, I'd like to talk to you about something," Lew said.

"Sure man, shoot," he replied with slurred speech.

"Our kids have been friends for over two years now, and my daughter tells me that they are boyfriend and girlfriend, whatever that means to kids that age."

"Oh, right, that boy has taken quite a shine to your girl. She is a pretty little thing, looks just like her mother."

"I'm aware of that, Mark," Lew said. "And if they stay friends in the future then it's likely that our two families might spend more time together and have more family outings like this from time to time."

"Well, I sure hope so, Lew, because I sure enjoyed this today."

"What I want to ask you, Mark, is that you don't ever come to my house again drunk. If you can agree to that, then I think we'll be good."

"I didn't mean to get out of line, Lew. I hope I didn't offend anyone."

"Mark, I'm sure you're a nice guy, but drinking changes who a person is. That's why I stopped drinking years ago and why I never drink in front of my family. A man turns into someone else when he's drunk."

"Did I curse too much? If I did, I'm really sorry.

"You did a few times, but that isn't what prompted this conversation."

"What was that, Lew?"

"All afternoon you kept watching my wife's ass like a dog watching one of those steaks."

"Oh," Mark said, "I'm sorry about that, Lew."

"Just don't come to my house again drunk, Mark, and we'll be okay."

ഗ്ര

Abby signed up for the fall semester of 'ninety-seven at the University of Colorado in The Springs. Her schedule permitted her to take Jamie Lynn to school in the mornings, before her classes began and to pick her up in the afternoon and take her home. The school was less than a mile from their house on Westmoreland Road.

Lew had exercised his option to buy the house in the second year after they had rented it. He put the house in joint ownership with Abby's name being on the title along with his. And now he was encouraging her to go back to school and get her nursing degree. Abby was curious as to why he seemed so insistent on her taking that step, but she didn't question him about it. She knew the man well enough to trust that his motive was in her and Jamie Lynn's best interests.

ഗ്ര

"How is school going?" Lew asked Abby.

"It's going well, I'm trying to keep my GPA up to at least my high school level, but it's hard. There's so much more to learn. They impress upon us the need to get at least six hours sleep a night, which doesn't seem difficult but I have lots of work to do at home."

"Six hours seems reasonable to me," he said.

"I'm lucky, though, some of the other students have

to work part time jobs. They try to get by with less sleep, and it really does affect their class and lab time."

"That's why I want you to go now while you don't have to work," he said.

"Are you going to leave me, Lew?" Abby asked him.

"I'm thinking that one day you will leave *me*, Abby."

"I'm not thinking that," she said. "Why would you think that?"

"I don't know, it's just a feeling I guess. I'm thirty-six-years-old, getting gray and putting on weight around the middle. And you're still just as beautiful as you were the day I met you. You look like you're aging in reverse."

Abby chuckled at that. "The gray hair on the sides is distinguished looking, I think," she told him. "And your job contributes to the weight gain. Maybe you should go to the gym more often. You can work that off if you dedicate yourself to it."

"I just don't have the energy to exercise that much anymore."

"Is that why you don't make love to me anymore?"

"It's not because I don't want to, Abby. It just feels like, when we do it, you're pretending you're with someone else. I'm sorry, I didn't mean that. It seems like you're pretending you're with Jamie."

"Oh, God, Lew," she said, crestfallen, "I don't consciously do that. I don't mean to make you feel like that."

"I know, Abby. We went into this marriage with our eyes open. We both knew that the two of us had wounds in our hearts that might not ever heal. I see you sometimes just sitting there deep in thought, and I know you are thinking about him. And I can't fault you because I have some days when my mind drifts back to my time with Peggy, and I do the same thing."

She sighed. "It's just that lately, for some reason, I've been having strong feelings—fantasy is probably a better word for it—but feelings that Jamie is still alive. I know it can't be true. Nobody can survive six months in the mountains in the winter. But I indulge in it, and it throws me into depression."

"Why don't you go to his parents and talk to them? Take Jamie Lynn, you know they'd love to see her."

"I couldn't do that, Lew, after all this time. I feel so terrible for leaving like I did without going to see them. If I go back now, they'd hate me."

"But perhaps it would ease your mind a bit, and Jamie Lynn would have grandparents she's never known."

"I just couldn't. I don't have the courage to do that."

☙❧

PPE, Personal Protective Equipment, Doctor Allen Parkins, announced their instructor for that day. "Gloves," he said, "you must always wear your gloves. Gloves do more than just protect you from diseases. For instance, when dealing with nitroglycerin, which is a commonly used treatment for patients experiencing chest pain, nurses must be extra careful when handling it. However, it can actually cause you to have a bowel movement if it makes contact with your skin as the result of a vasovagal reaction."

The student sitting next to Abby, a woman named Lillian, leaned over. "How would you like to be working on a guy having a heart attack and all of a sudden you shit in your pants?" Abby laughed out loud.

Doctor Parkins overheard and called out, "What's funny back there, Lillian?"

"I was just telling Abby that it would be embarrassing to be treating someone having a heart attack and shit in your pants." The whole class burst into laughter.

Doctor Parkins smiled slightly. "Yes, that would be a bit awkward," he said, keeping a straight face. "CPR masks. Some of you, who may be squeamish, should consider using a CPR mask when administering CPR to a patient. Face masks. Face masks will keep blood and other bodily fluids from entering your mouths when treating patients."

The doctor then launched into a general lecture on the nursing program that Abby's class had signed up for. "You all have associate nursing degrees, as I understand it, having attended a two-year college prior to coming to UCCS.Being a nurse is really hard work. I don't think anyone will argue with that, but it is very rewarding work. And I don't just mean monetarily. There is a reason people talk about the challenges of nursing—time management and constantly being faced with one mini crisis after another. There are so many things that can put a lot of pressure on a student. Sometimes that even includes emotional trauma. But it is all worth it in the end to have an in-demand career that actually helps heal others and improves the lives of strangers. And I didn't mention an amazing support system of experienced nurses to help you all the way. I'd like to ask the class if you have had any experiences, in your time here, that you'd like to share with us."

Abby raised her hand.

"Okay, Ms…"

"Abby Morgan."

"Abby Morgan," the doctor said. "Proceed, Ms. Morgan."

"Well, the first couple of times I ate lunch with some of my fellow students, they started talking shop and mentioning bodily fluids, bed sores, puss, and blood, and such, I started gagging and thought I was going to throw up. But after about a week, I just went on eating my sandwich and ignored it all."

There was a chorus of agreement all over the classroom. And the doctor nodded knowingly. "Good, thank you, Ms. Morgan, for ruining my lunch." Everyone laughed at that.

"Now. I'm going to go over what you can expect and hope to achieve while you are in our nursing program here at UCCS. You will have to take extensive notes. If I go too fast, just raise your hand, and I will slow down a bit.

"Bachelor's Degree Programs: An aspiring RN can earn a bachelor of science in nursing, BSN, in four years at a college or university. If you already have an associates degree, you can enroll in an RN to BSN program which is geared specifically for those who have an associate's degree or nursing diploma. This path usually takes about two to three years. Your typical course load will consist of bioethics, fundamentals of microbiology, nursing, research, nursing care of the older adult, and public health nursing.

"An associate's degree in nursing—AND—includes courses in anatomy, nursing, nutrition, chemistry, and microbiology, among others. You'll also be required to take general liberal arts classes. Earning an ADN is the most popular option for registered nurses and opens the door to entry-level staff nurse positions which will provide you with hands-on experience in the medical field. This is the fastest path to becoming a registered nurse as most associate's degree programs last about two to three years. If you are attending full time, then the two-year time frame is a more accurate estimate of your time commitment.

"After completing your degree program, you'll need to take the National Council Licensure Examination, which you will see abbreviated as NCLEX. In order to sit for the exam, you'll need to apply for a nursing license from your state board of nursing. Since each state has different eligibility criteria, check with your state board to ensure you've met the requirements in order to take the exam.

"The NCLEX exam covers four categories of needs, according to the National Council of State Boards of Nursing: safe, effective care environment—management care and safety and infection control; psychosocial integrity—coping and adaptation and psychosocial adaptation; health promotion and maintenance—growth and development through the life span and prevention and early detection of disease; and physiology integrity—basic care and comfort, pharmacological and parenteral therapies, reduction of risk potential, and physiological adaptation.

"Okay, I hope you got all that. I can provide a printed version of the entire lecture if that will be helpful to you. Thank you, you are dismissed."

"It sounds a lot more complicated than it is," Lillian said to Abby, as they were leaving the classroom."

"I certainly hope so, because that all seems very hard, and I really want to do this."

"I have to do this," Lillian said, "I need the money. I have two kids to support and a deadbeat ex-husband who won't help support them."

"I'm sorry, Lillian," Abby said.

"What's your situation?"

Abby was almost embarrassed to tell her. "My husband is a psychology professor here at UCCS. He encouraged me to come back and finish getting my degree so I'd have that to fall back on in case something happened to him."

"Does he have a death premonition or something?" Lillian asked.

"I don't know, I thought that was kind of strange, too, but I liked the idea."

"We'll have to talk more about this, but I have to go pick up my kids from school, take them to my mother's, and get to work."

"Yeah, me too," Abby said. "I have to pick up my daughter from school."

❧❧❧

"So, what did you learn in school today, Mom?" Jamie Lynn asked.

"Are you getting even with me for all the times I asked you that?"

"No, I am genuinely interested in your career, Mom, but it is a nice role reversal experiment."

"Well, today, I learned about peripherally inserted central catheters, or more commonly called PICC lines."

"Wow, that's a mouthful," Jamie Lynn said. "What does it mean?"

"PICC lines are small, flexible tubes that are inserted through the arm and terminate in the chest, essentially acting as a catheter for the heart. This is a procedure that can be scary for a nurse to learn. We have to measure where to start the line and estimate how long the line needs to be to end up close to the patient's heart. We practice on dummies. I haven't practiced on a live person yet."

"That's serious business, Mom. I never thought much about what nurses really do."

"Is nursing something you think you might want to do for a career, honey?"

"I don't know. I haven't really given it much thought. I'm going to marry Tommy one day when we get out of school."

"You're eleven-years-old, daughter, don't you think you're a little young to be thinking about getting married?"

"No, I promised Tommy I'd marry him when we're old enough."

"Okay, well, I also learned about scabies. Do you know what that is?"

"No, I never heard of that. What is it?

"It's a disease, and I had never heard of it either, but it's an infestation of microscopic mites that burrow under the skin. Nasty business."

"How can you remember all this stuff you have to know, Mom? It seems like too much."

"I just hope I can, honey. It's a lot of stuff, all right," Abby said. "Everything we learn is important to the job, though."

εɔɕɔ

In nineteen-ninety-eight, Abby completed her class-work and training to get her BSN and graduated with a 3.6 GPA. It was not as high as the 3.8 she had maintained in high school but "Not too shabby," Lew told her.

"I'm happy with it," she said. "I'm getting some offers from local hospitals for a job. What do you think I should do?"

"Do you want to go to work?"

"Yes, I'd kind of like to go back to work. I'd like to put away some money for Jamie Lynn's college, if she ever decides on what she wants to do, besides marry Tommy Baker."

"Then why don't you take the best offer and put all your money in a savings account, except for some personal money you may want to spend on yourself and Jamie Lynn. I think that would be a great idea."

"I can help out with the bills, Lew. I'd like to."

"I don't need the help, Abby. I'd rather you saved your money."

Abby went for an interview at Eisenhower Hospital, in Colorado Springs, and accepted their offer of a $45,000 base salary a year. She called her friend Lillian from school and told her that the hospital was still in need of nurses, and Lillian made an appointment to come in for an interview.

Abby couldn't shake the nagging feeling that Lew

seemed obsessed with her becoming financially independent. He had encouraged her to get her nursing degree, and, now that she had done that, he was encouraging her to get a job and save all her money for herself. Whatever his motives, they were certainly not an attempt to exploit her and live off her earnings while he lay around, enjoying life.

Lew was making six figures at his job and was generous with his support of her and Jamie Lynn. They basically wanted for nothing. Not a day went by that Abby didn't realize how fortunate she was that she had married Lew Morgan. He was a good dad and a good husband. And, had she not lost the only man she would ever truly love, Lew could have been the love of her life. Now he seemed to be slowly working his way out of her life, preparing her for the day when that would happen.

She wasn't sure how she felt about that. She couldn't imagine "dating" again or ever falling in love. She didn't even think she could ever feel about another man the way she felt about Lew. And she knew there would never be another Jamie in her life. So, if Lew ever asked that they separate, she didn't know what she would do.

It was at the end of the year 2000, when Lew came to Abby and told her of his desire for their life together. "I need to talk to you, Abby," he said. "Can we go out on the patio?"

"Of course, Lew," she said, with a sense of foreboding.

Abby sat down, and Lew pulled up a chair facing her. "First, I want to say, Abby, that you have been a wonderful wife to me, and I love you very much."

"I love you too, Lew."

"I know, and I know we've talked about the other two burdens in our lives. I know you think about Jamie quite a bit, and I understand that. You've been very honest with me. I appreciate your honesty, but you can't know how much it hurts."

"I'm sorry, Lew, I'm so sorry," Abby said.

"No, I understand. The first few years of our marriage, I had the same thoughts about Peggy. But the more I fell in love with you, the less and less I thought about her."

"Oh, Lew, I didn't know. I'm so selfish."

"No, Abby, you're not selfish. You're the most honest person I know. You loved a man, and I don't think you'll ever get over him."

Abby burst into tears.

"I know now that I can never fill that void," Lew said. "You've given me fourteen wonderful years, you gave me a wonderful daughter that I love more than anything in this world. I wouldn't trade our time together for anything, Abby."

"Don't leave me, Lew," she said, tears welling up in her eyes.

"I have to, Abby. I have to find someone who isn't in love with a dead man. I need someone who will love me and only me. I hope you can understand that."

"What are we going to tell Jamie Lynn?" Abby asked him, still crying.

"We'll need to think on that, I guess. I don't want her to think we hate each other."

"I'll never hate you, Lew, you've been wonderful to me."

"Perhaps you can explain it to her, better than I can."

"I won't lie to her, Lew. I'm going to be just as honest with her as you were with me."

Lew nodded. "Okay, that makes sense. Now, I want you to have this house, you and Jamie Lynn. You make enough money to support yourself. The payments on the house are fairly low, your car is paid for. You should get by okay. If you need money, just call me."

"We'll be fine, Lew. You're more than generous. Thank you for encouraging me to go back to school and preparing me for this."

"I just don't want you to have any hardships. I want our daughter to have every opportunity to pursue whatever goals she decides to pursue."

"I'm so grateful for you, Lew," Abby said. "You've been good to us for all this time that we've been married. I feel like I've let you down, and I'm so sorry."

"You can't help how you feel. I won't say we can be friends, Abby, that's such a cliché. I think I will always love you, but I want to be a part of Jamie Lynn's life. She's still my daughter."

"Of course, Lew, nothing will ever change that."

Jamie Lynn was heartbroken and didn't understand, when Abby told her about the divorce. In her mind, her parents had a perfect marriage.

"I guess I can understand how much you loved my biological father. You were soul mates. You found that one in a lifetime love that is never lost. I'll never understand why life has to be so cruel, but God gave us a consolation prize when he gave you my daddy, Lew. I don't know now if I can ever believe in true love."

"My God, honey," Abby said, hugging her daughter tightly. "How did you ever get so wise?"

"I got it from you, Mom," she said.

Nights alone were an emotional roller coaster for Abby, with Lew gone. She now reached across the bed and felt nothing but empty sheets. Years before, in the twilight just before she fell asleep, she would reach out for Jamie and feel Lew lying beside her. But Lew was flesh and blood lying there, and Jamie was only a memory. He was a memory she could now reach for without guilt and without hurting a man who loved her.

Chapter 7

A Red-Haired Girl

2002:

Jamie Lynn turned sixteen in November and had become a carbon copy of her mother, Abby. The red hair she wore slightly longer than her mother's but her face was just as pretty, Abby's face, seemed to defy the effects of her thirty-six years of life and the turmoil it had brought her and still turned men's heads everywhere she went. Mother and daughter could wear each other's clothes, being the same height and build. Both had light skin with pink undertones and were often mistaken for each other at a distance.

Two months before she turned sixteen, Jamie Lynn began her junior year at Doherty High School, in Colorado Springs, in September of 2002.

"Hi, what's your name?" a boy asked her, on the first day of school.

"I'm Jamie Lynn Morgan," she said, smiling. "Who are you?"

"Jerry Beamer," the boy said. "I was wondering if maybe you would go to a movie with me some Saturday."

"Thanks, Jerry, but I have a boyfriend."

"I should have known. Who is he?"

"His name is Tommy Baker," she said.

"Oh, that crazy bastard," the boy said, shaking his head. "Well, if you ever break up with him, let me know first, okay?"

"Okay," she said, laughing.

A little farther down the hall, another boy approached her.

"Hey, beautiful, what's your name?" he asked her.

"I have a boyfriend," Jamie Lynn said.

The boy just waved and walked on. "Snooty bitch," he mumbled to himself.

Jamie Lynn saw the familiar gait of Tommy Baker coming down the hall. As always, he was in a hurry. The boy always seemed to be in a hurry. Ever since his parents divorced, he had become obsessed with making his way in the world. He took Drivers Ed, as soon as the state would allow it, and got his license as soon as he was of legal age. At one time, he held three part-time jobs at the same time. Unlike his irresponsible father, Mark Baker, Tommy saved his money. He was determined to make something of himself one day.

"Hey, baby, have you got your schedule yet?" he said, as he walked up to her.

"Yes," she said and handed it to him.

"Home Room, Gordon, she's okay, I had her last year. Fifth period, Colorado History, McNasty. He's an asshole."

"McNasty?"

"McNally is his real name. I didn't get along with him very well."

"Well, that's a shocker. You get along so well with everyone else in the world."

Tommy smiled broadly. "You know, you're the only one who can rag on me like that. I can't get mad at you. Anybody hit on you yet today?"

"No," she said.

"I'm surprised, you're the best-looking girl in this school. They will before the day is over," he said.

"I'll tell them I belong to you, Tommy."

"I love you, Jamie Lynn. You're the only thing in my life that makes any sense."

"I love you too, Tommy. You're the only thing in *my* life that doesn't make any sense."

"That's a hell of a thing to say. What do you mean?"

"A boy asked me to go to a movie with him and, when I told him you were my boyfriend, he said you were a crazy bastard."

"That's a compliment, baby," Tommy said.

"I know, and that's what makes no sense. I don't know why I love you. You've got this crazy streak in you that intrigues me most of the time but scares me sometimes."

"Who was the guy? I'll go kick his ass."

"Yeah, that's what I'm talking about."

Jamie Lynn couldn't identify the exact date and time when she and Tommy Baker fell in love, but she knew it happened for both of them pretty much at the same time. She believed it was when she was ten and he was eleven, but it might have been earlier or slightly later in their lives.

All she was sure of was that she could not remember a time when she was not in love with Tommy. She had held him in her arms on numerous occasions, like the times when his father had slapped him around and humiliated him.

Tommy resented his father all his life, for the man's mistreatment of him and for his abuse of Tommy's mother, but Tommy had not let the anger seethe inside him, He had prepared himself with body-building, boxing, and martial arts. And it was on a date with Jamie Lynn that his life of abuse by his father reached a point of confrontation. It was in August of 2002.

"I got a new Denver Broncos bedspread I want to show you before we go to the movie," Tommy said. "Okay?"

"Sure," Jamie Lynn said. "You're not just trying to get me in your bedroom, are you?"

"No, "he said. "If that was my intention, I'd stop the car and get down on my knees and beg like a dog."

She started giggling and patted the top of his head, "Good boy."

"Oh, yeah, rub it in."

"I'm sorry, Tommy, I just want to wait until we're married."

"Well, we can do it again after we get married, lots of times."

She just stared at him.

"Never mind," he said. "Forget I mentioned it."

When they arrived at the Baker house, Tommy saw his dad's car in the driveway.

"Now what's this asshole doing here?" he said. "You wait here."

"No, Tommy, I want to go with you. I don't want you to have trouble with your dad."

"Okay," he said, "but don't say anything to him."

❧❧❧

"I didn't know you were going to be here today, Pop. Does Mom know you're here?"

"I came over to talk to her. Why are you here so early?"

"I just dropped by to show Jamie Lynn my new Broncos bedspread."

"You gonna show her the sheets too?" Baker said.

"Don't disrespect my girl like that, Pop, I don't appreciate it, and she doesn't deserve it."

"Ooh wee," the older man said, leering at Jamie Lynn. "You've grown up some since I last saw you. You look just like that pretty mother of yours."

"Shut your damned mouth, Pop, don't talk to her like that." Tommy scolded him.

Baker was drunk and apparently unable to use what little good sense he might have possessed at one time. "What are you gonna do if I don't, boy?"

"I'm gonna kick your ass, that's what I'm gonna do."

"You really think you can kick my ass?"

"I *know* I can kick your ass," Tommy shouted back at him.

"Well, you got the *talking* down," Baker said.

Before he could say another word, Tommy had closed the gap between them. He was throwing punches before his dad had time to react. Tommy knocked him to the floor and then straddled him and continued to pummel him. He most likely would have beaten the man to death had Jamie Lynn not grabbed him, held his arms, and begged him to stop.

"You'll kill him, Tommy, then where will you be?

Come on, let's go to my daddy's apartment. My daddy will know what to do."

As they were about to leave the Baker house, Tommy stopped his car. "I forgot something," he said, "I'll be right back." He got out and ran into the house. He returned in just a couple of minutes with his Broncos bedspread. "Can you keep this for me for a while?"

"Of course, I will," Jamie Lynn said.

露

"Well, according to the way you described it to me," Lew said, "technically you hit him first, but he was verbally abusive to Jamie Lynn, and you believed he was going to assault you. You did believe he was going to assault you, didn't you, Tommy?"

"Yes, sir, and I was afraid he might hurt Jamie Lynn, so I went after him. It was a pre-emptive strike, so to speak."

Jamie Lynn started giggling. Both Lew and Tommy looked at her and laughed at her seemingly uncontrolled giggling then looked at each other and laughed again.

"I think you should call your mother," Lew said. "Mark violated your mother's restraining order, and she might want to notify the authorities."

"I'll call her at work, so she doesn't go home and find him there, not knowing ahead of time."

"If you need to, you can stay here with me tonight. I

have an extra room. Check with your mother before you go back home."

"Okay, Mr. Morgan, thank you," Tommy said. "I need to talk to Jamie Lynn about something, if it's okay with you."

"I'm sure that would be fine, Tommy," Lew replied. "Why don't you two go sit on my patio?"

"Oh, sure, Mr. Morgan, that's fine," Tommy said."

"This isn't about that army thing again, is it, Tommy?" Jamie Lynn asked him as they sat down on the patio.

Tommy nodded. "It is," he said. "Ever since nine-eleven, I've had this feeling nagging inside me that I should be over there doing my part."

"But you said you would wait until you finished high school."

"I know I did but that's two more years, and it might be over by then."

"Good, I hope it is," she yelled at him, "then you wouldn't have to go. People get killed in war."

"But this thing with my dad is just going to get worse and my mom. My mom is not a mean drunk, like my dad, but she's still an alcoholic. The only good thing in my life is you and your family. I just need to get away from here and make something of myself."

"You're already something to me," she said."

"Will you wait for me, Jamie Lynn, and marry me when I come back?"

"You know I will. You don't even have to ask me that."

"I think you're making a mistake, Tommy," Lew told him, "but I admire your sense of patriotism. I just hope you'll call Jamie Lynn regularly because she's very fond of you, and I know she's going to worry about you, a lot."

"I love her, Mr. Morgan. We plan on getting married when I get back."

"Well, I can't say that surprises me, Tommy. I mean, you've been going steady since you were in diapers, practically."

Tommy laughed. "A long time, that's for sure, Mr. Morgan."

"For gosh sake, Tommy, call me Lew. You're a grown man now. If you can serve the country in combat, you can at least call me by my first name."

"Lew, it is," Tommy said. "Thank you, Lew."

જ્જિજ્

Tommy dropped out of school at seventeen and joined the Army. The boy was far more intelligent than anyone had ever given him credit for and his ASVAB—Armed Services Vocational Aptitude Battery—test scores were among the highest of any in his time segment. That fact and his being from Colorado facilitated his transfer to the 10th Mountain Division, which was currently engaged in the hostilities in Afghanistan.

Operation Anaconda took place in early March of 2002 in the Shahi-Kot Valley and Arma Mountains, southeast of the town of Zurmat which was 151 killometers—roughly 95 miles—from Kabul. This operation was the first large-scale battle in the US War in Afghanistan since the Battle of Tora Bora in December of 2001.

Between March 2, 2002 and March 16, 2002 ,1,700 airlifted US troops and 1,000 pro-government Afghan militia battled between 300 and 1,000 Al Qaeda and Taliban fighters to obtain control of the valley. The Taliban and Al Qaeda forces fired mortars and heavy machine guns from entrenched positions in the caves and ridges of the mountainous terrain at the US forces attempting to secure the area.

Intelligence indicated that a strong presence of Taliban and Al Qaeda fighters. Approximately 150 to 200 were believed to be wintering in the valley, preparing for a spring offensive. Plans were drawn up to assault the Shahi-Kot Valley using Afghan military forces, assisted by US special operations.

The plan called for an attack on the valley, along with units positioned in the mountains to the east to prevent any escape into Pakistan.

Expectations were that fighters, as in the case of Tora Bora several months earlier, would flee in the face of an assault and that blocker groups would simply be able to round them up.

The US forces involved consisted of the 187th Infantry Regiment of the 101st Airborne Division and soldiers of 1st Battalion, 87th Infantry Regiment, 10th Mountain Division. It was with this unit that PFC Tommy Baker would experience his first taste of combat in Afghanistan.

His platoon had been airlifted to its position on the windswept slopes of the Arma Mountains. Their orders were to set up observation posts and report on any activity by hostile forces that might be on the move in the area.

When the Chinook left, Tommy felt the awful sensation of being as alone as he had ever been in his entire life. The sergeant of his sixteen-man squad, Gerald Parker from Helena, Montana, ordered them to move up the mountain. They had only gone a couple hundred yards when they received a round of sniper fire that struck the backpack of one soldier but did no damage to the man. Everyone hit the ground and sought cover behind the nearest rocks. "Don't anyone return fire," Sergeant Parker shouted. "Anybody see where it came from?"

"I saw it," Tommy said, pointing up the mountain at a ledge beneath two large rock outcroppings. "It looks like he's set up in that little cubby hole right below those two big rocks about two-hundred yards up."

Parker looked with his binoculars. "You sure that's where it came from, Baker? I can't see him."

"I am, Sarge. I saw the flash."

"Okay, everybody, stay put. Let me think for a minute." He called for an airstrike but was told there were none available at the time and that he should just wait. Parker kept looking with his glasses but still could not see the enemy sniper. He didn't want to risk moving out and losing a man, so he decided to wait a while longer.

"Sarge," Tommy said, "look up to the left over here. There's a path that goes up and around the sniper's position. I can snake my way up there, get behind him, and take him out."

"I don't know what's up there, Baker. There may be more of them."

"Well, what the hell are we going to do? We can't lay here on our asses all night long, we'll freeze to death. If we try to leave, he'll shoot some of us."

Parker took a long look at the left side of their position and then back up at the sniper's lair. "Okay, Baker," he said. "But if you run into any more of them, you get your ass back down here, and we'll wait for an airstrike."

"Right, Sarge," Tommy said. "Now, it may take me an hour or so. Don't watch me or even look to the left side while I'm moving. If he is watching our position with binoculars and sees everybody looking up to the left, he'll figure out what's going on."

"Okay, Baker, but you be careful, you hear me?"

"Careful is my middle name, Sarge," Tommy said.

"Crazy is more like it," Parker replied.

At some points along the path, Tommy was able walk or low creep, and at some other locations, he had to crawl to keep from being observed. It was an hour and a half before he reached the top of the ridge where the sniper was positioned.

There were no other hostiles in the area as far as he could tell. He estimated that he was approximately a hundred yards from the target.

The area looked much different from on top than it had looked from their position below. He had to move slowly and stay near the edge of the ridge for fear of walking right past the target. But soon, he came to what looked like the two major rock formations that guarded the sniper's firing platform. Tommy crawled over to the edge and risked a peek. There were two of them in the cubby hole, and they seemed to be going in and out of a cave behind them. Tommy started talking to himself now. He had to plan what to do about this.

One of them had disappeared into the cave, if that's what it was. It could be just a depression in the rocks. Maybe there were only two. If there was a cave, there might be a lot more of them. Well, it didn't matter, he had to kill them all, no matter how many there were.

The second man stepped back into his view, so he aimed his rifle, shot one of them in the back of the head, and then quickly shot the other one. Neither man ever knew what hit him. There was a chorus of voices babbling from within the rocks below. "It's a fucking cave," Tommy said out loud, as men started running out. He began firing quickly and killed six more of them before they stopped coming out. Then he dropped a grenade down at the mouth of the cave, or where he judged the mouth of the cave to be, just for good measure.

The rest of his squad, having heard the firing, was heading up the mountain toward him and arrived about the same time that he found a way down from the top of the ridge to the cave.

"Fuck me, Baker," Sergeant Parker said. "That was some mighty fine soldiering, thank you."

"They were stupid bastards," Tommy said. "Shouldn't kill people that stupid. They could help us win the war."

"What do you mean?

"If they had just let us come on up the hill, they could have killed us all. When the guy fired that shot, he signed their death warrant."

"You're fucking right. I hadn't thought of that. I hope they are all that stupid."

"I do too," Tommy said.

A week later, Tommy's unit was air lifted out of the Shahi-Kot Valley and taken back to Bagram Air base. "Don't seem like we did very much to get a vacation, Sarge," Tommy told Sergeant Parker.

"We played a vital role in Operation Anaconda, Baker," Parker replied "Our squad killed eight of the enemy. If we don't count the ones you killed, we didn't kill any."

"Don't matter who kills the bastards, as long as they get killed," Tommy said, and Sergeant Parker started laughing. "What's so funny, Sarge?" Tommy asked.

"That's what I told the captain when he congratulated me for the unit killing eight Taliban. I told him that, if we don't count the ones killed by PFC Baker, the unit didn't kill any Taliban. That was the captain's position, Baker, his very words. He said it doesn't matter who kills the enemy as long as they end up dead."

⋯

Tommy waited with anticipation as the second ring ended and then the phone picked up and Jamie Lynn's voice answered. "Hello," she said.

"Hi, baby, how are you?"

"Tommy, ohmygosh, Tommy, where are you?"

"I'm still in Afghanistan," he said. "I bought one of those pre-paid phone cards to call you with. I'm at Bagram Air Base. It's really good to hear your voice."

"Oh, you too. I miss you so much. Are you being careful?"

"Yeah, sure, it's actually pretty boring here. I've doing a lot of guard duty and training. It's not much fun."

"Good," Jamie said, "because I know what you army guys mean by fun. I hope you can stay out of it. I just want you to get back home in one piece."

"I'm told we'll be coming back to the States, maybe in July."

"Oh, Tommy, that would be wonderful. Where will you be stationed, do you know?"

"Not yet. I'll let you know when I know more. I gotta go, baby. I love you."

"I love you too, Tommy, call me whenever you can."

A week later their platoon was airlifted back to the Shahi-Kot Valley to support two SEAL fire teams that were to be inserted in order to establish observation points on either end of the valley. One team was to move to a peak called Takur Ghar, which commanded the southern approach to the valley. The plan was for that team, by helicopter insertion, to reach the peak by dawn on March third. Tommy's platoon would be in position prior to the SEAL team's arrival.

The first SEAL team was picked up by an MF-47 on March third at around twenty-three-hundred hours, but the Chinook experienced engine problems, and they had to wait for a replacement helicopter to arrive to transport the SEALs. This delay meant that the SEAL team could not be inserted into the LZ to the east of the peak until oh-two-thirty on March fourth, which would not give them enough time to reach the peak before daylight. The decision was made to insert directly on the peak at around oh-three-hundred.

The Chinook attempted to land on top of the mountain. As they approached, the helicopter was met with RPG fire. Two rocket-propelled grenades hit the ship, shutting down one of its engines, the electric system, and the hydraulic system. The helicopter was forced to crash land in the valley below.

The platoon from the 10th Mountain Division came under attack by Taliban fighters after the SEAL team had abandoned Takur Ghar. "Look alive," Sergeant Parker said. "Make each shot count. Baker, take three men and guard our left flank."

"Parilli, Morris, Cooper, come with me," Tommy told them, as he ran behind some rock formations to the left of their position. A group of about fifteen hostiles were working their way toward the American positions, weaving in and out from behind one rock to another, in an apparent attempt to flank them on the left side. "Make your shots count," Tommy said, and the four men opened up on the approaching enemy, repelling them, and killing at least five or six while taking no casualties.

Second Squad had one man killed and three wounded. First Squad—Tommy Baker's squad—had two men wounded. The dead and wounded were medevacked out within hours. The Chinooks came in the next day and extracted the rest of the platoon and airlifted them back to Bagram. In July, they received word that they were shipping out, back to the States.

"So that's it, Sarge?" Tommy asked Parker.

"What do you mean, Baker?"

"Is that all the combat we're going to see? Hell, I got in more fights in high school."

Parker laughed. "I have no doubt you did, Baker, but

they weren't shooting at you in high school, were they?"

"Some of them would have if they could."

"Just consider us lucky that our squad didn't lose any people, and that's mostly thanks to you."

"I'm glad of that," Tommy said. "We have been lucky."

"And, by the way, after I filed my report with the captain after our first scuffle in the valley, he put you in for a medal for killing those eight Taliban."

"No shit?"

"Nope, I don't know when or what will happen, but they'll let you know."

"How much money is that worth?"

Parker chuckled. "Probably get you free beer every so often."

Tommy shrugged. "Better than a sharp stick in the eye, as my old man used to say."

⸙⸙⸙

"You lied to me, Tommy," Jamie Lynn shouted at him over the phone.

"What are you talking about, baby?" Tommy replied, confused.

"There's an article in the paper here about you. It says you won a Bronze Star for valor in combat. You told me it was boring for you over there. You said you were just sitting around doing nothing, or almost nothing, and now I find you've been in the fighting."

"Aw, hell, Jamie, that's mostly just a bunch of bullshit."

"Daddy said it's a big deal. He said the Bronze Star with the 'V' for valor means you risked your life to save your buddies."

"Your daddy is a school teacher. He doesn't know anything about what goes on over here. The media blows these things up, all out of proportion. Stop worrying."

"I can't stop worrying. What am I going to do if something happens to you?"

"Relax, Jamie," he told her. "I'm pretty much done here. We're shipping out in a couple of days. I'm transferring to an infantry division so I can finish out my tour at Fort Carson. I should be back in The Springs in a month or so, maybe sooner."

"Oh, thank God for that. I'll be so happy to see you."

えりくり

Tommy was waiting at the main gate when Jamie Lynn arrived to pick him up. He was pacing up and down when he spotted her and came running to her car.

"Hi, baby," he said, "thanks for coming to get me. Come here, let me kiss you."

She slid out from behind the steering wheel, and he began kissing her, passionately, like a man who had not eaten in a very long time. When his right hand moved to her breasts, she grabbed it and pushed him away. "Stop that Tommy," she said.

"I'm sorry, baby, if you weren't so damned good looking—"

"Maybe you should have gotten you an ugly girlfriend," she said.

"But I fell in love with you, Jamie Lynn, now I'm stuck."

"Well, that's one way to put it, I guess."

"I didn't mean it like that. Let's go to my house. I told my mom I'd come by and see her."

At the Bakers' house, Tommy's mother was not at home, so Tommy again directed his pent-up sexual passion toward Jamie Lynn. He began kissing her again. "I missed you, baby," he said. "You can't imagine how much I missed you."

"If the bulge in your pants is any indication, then I'd say you missed me quite a lot," she said and giggled. "You wanna put that thing away so you can think with your other head?"

"All right," he said. "In the zone, I had to hide your picture in my locker to keep every swinging dick in my unit from trying to take it into the latrine with them."

"Why would they do that?"

"Now, why do you think?"

"Oh," she said and started giggling again. "Did you ever take it into the latrine with you?"

"You don't wanna know stuff like that, but I was worried what was gonna wear out first, my hand or my pecker."

"Oh, my gosh, Tommy, men are so crude."

"Come on, baby," he said, "give me some loving." He kissed her again, and she felt herself getting aroused, so she pushed him away.

"You promised me, Tommy. You promised me that you would not pressure me to have sex before we're married."

"Then let's get married, now."

"You know my mom and dad won't let me get married at sixteen. I'm not going to get married before I get out of high school just so you can screw me."

"It wouldn't be just for that, Jamie, it would be because I love you, and I do want to spend the rest of my life with you. You're just so damned beautiful."

"Maybe I should just go home," she said.

He sighed, and his demeanor suddenly changed. "Maybe we should take some time off, Jamie."

"What do you mean?" she asked him.

"I mean you need to decide if you want to be a woman or a nun."

"You're breaking up with me?"

"I just need some time to think things out. Come on, Jamie Lynn, we're past the hand holding stage. I need you. Everybody does it nowadays. Why do you have to be so prudish?"

"It's special to me, Tommy. I've wanted to marry you for as long as I've known you, but I want it to be the real thing. I don't want us to be like everyone else."

"You wouldn't be here if your mother hadn't screwed your dad before they were married, so don't try and sound so self-righteous."

"Oh, you go to hell, Tommy Baker. My mother was going to marry my dad when he was lost. And she wasn't still in high school. Their relationship was not cheap, and don't you ever say it was."

She stormed out of his house, slamming the door behind her, got into her car, and drove home.

When Abby came home from work, she found Jamie Lynn in her room, lying on her bed crying her eyes out.

"What's wrong, honey," she asked. "Are you okay? What happened?"

"Tommy broke up with me, Mom."

"Oh, honey, I'm sorry," Abby said. "Did you two have a fight?"

"He broke up with me because I won't have sex with him."

Abby looked at her daughter for a full minute. Tears came to her eyes.

"I'm so proud of you, darling. I'm so thankful that you're my daughter. You just don't know how proud I am to be your mother."

"What am I going to do, Mom? I love Tommy."

"Keep doing what you're doing, honey, and keep being who you are. The boy will come to his senses in time."

☙☙☙

The boy, Tommy Baker, was almost eighteen and was, by all reasoning, a man who was still dating a sixteen-year-old girl. By virtue of their birthdates, he would turn eighteen in February of 2003, while she would not be seventeen until November of that year.

He was still a boy in the purest sense of the word, but a boy who had been to war and had distinguished himself in combat.

He had taken action that had undoubtedly saved the lives of many of his fellow soldiers.

After rotating back to the States from Afghanistan, Tommy had proven to be a good soldier in an elite unit, the 10th Mountain Division.

He had been promoted to corporal and was being touted as good leadership material. He had foolishly, on a whim, broken up with the only girl he had ever dated in school and the only girl he knew he would ever love.

"Hey, Baker, when you going to marry that fox you been dating?" This was Jimmy Murdoch, one of Tommy's fellow soldiers in his unit.

"She's got a year left in high school yet," Tommy said. "Besides, I dumped her."

"Are you shittin' me?" Murdoch said. "Why in the world would you do that?"

"It's personal."

"How about giving me her number then?"

"Hey, man, don't fuck around. That's my girl," Tommy said.

"You just said you dumped her. You gotta be the dumbest bastard on the planet to dump that girl. Granted, all I've seen is her picture .but if she looks like her picture—"

"Shut the fuck up, Jimmy! Don't even think about calling my girl."

"Whoa, I'm sorry, man, I was just messin' with you. I just hope you work it out with her. She looks like a keeper to me."

ೞೞ

Tommy hesitated for a moment before knocking on Lew's apartment door. He wasn't quite sure what he was going to say. He knew it was a little crazy to talk to his girl's dad about getting back together with the man's daughter, but Tommy didn't know what else to do.

"Hey, Tommy, what's going on," Lew said when he opened the door.

"I need to talk to you for a minute, if you have the time, Lew," Tommy said.

"Of course, Tommy, come on in."

They sat down in his living room.

"I made a big mistake with Jamie."

"She told me you broke up with her," Lew said.

"She did?"

"She's pretty hurt, Tommy. Jamie Lynn loves you, and she's very loyal. I don't think she's ever even looked at another boy in all the time she's known you."

"Did she tell you why I did it?"

"No, but I have a pretty good idea. Why don't you tell me?"

"She's just so beautiful. When I'm with her, I can't keep my hands off her. I think I'm losing my mind."

"I know the symptoms, Tommy," Lew said. "I was your age once. Jamie Lynn is one of those rare girls who is committed to waiting until you're married before sleeping with you."

"I don't know what to do."

"Well, I'm not going to advise you to go find some other man's daughter to assuage your pent-up passion just to keep you from bothering mine, but if you make the sacrifice and wait until you're married, I guarantee you that you'll be happier about it down the road."

"I said something pretty hurtful to her, Lew."

"You want to tell me about it?"

"I told her that she wouldn't even be here if her mother hadn't screwed her father before they were married."

"Ouch, that's pretty harsh, all right, but men will say

almost anything when they're trying to get into a woman's pants. I'm not excusing what you said, don't get me wrong, but hormones can make a man do crazy things sometimes."

"Well, I can't go on without her, I know that. I need to apologize to her and get her back."

"She'll be spending the weekend with me. Do you want me to ask her if she wants to see you so you can apologize?"

"Would you do that, Lew?"

"Yes, Tommy, I will, but I have a plan. Here's what I have in mind…"

e∕ɔe∕ɔ

"Where are we going, Daddy?" Jamie Lynn asked him.

"I thought we might have a picnic in Cheyenne Canyon today, if that's okay with you, darling."

"Yes, I'd like that, thank you, Daddy."

"I brought a lot of stuff." He pointed to the back seat with his thumb. She turns and looked.

"Holy cow, I won't be able to eat all that," she said.

"I just wanted to make sure we had enough." He checked his watch. "Oh, I meant to tell you, Tommy came to see me the other day."

"He did?" She perked up a bit. "What did he want?"

"He wanted me to ask you if you'd be willing to sit

down with him and give him a chance to apologize."

"Tommy said that? Oh, Daddy, do you mean it, he really said that?"

"He said it, and he seemed very sincere. He said he loves you and always has. If you're willing to listen to him, I can arrange a meeting between the two of you." He checked his watch again.

"Yes," she said. "I would love for you to do that. Thank you, Daddy."

"Okay, but right now the order of the day is our picnic. We'll go to Helen Hunt Falls."

It was a short drive up the canyon to the falls. Lew turned into a space and cut off the engine.

"I'll get the basket," she said.

"Hold on a minute, darling, look up there on the bridge," he said, pointing at the bridge that spanned the crest of the falls.

She looked up and, there, standing at parade rest was Tommy Baker, in full dress summer uniform, looking down at them.

Jamie Lynn shrieked. "Oh, Daddy, you set this up, that's why you kept looking at your watch. You knew he was here waiting. Thank you, I love you." She jumped across the seat and hugged him around his neck. Then she got out of the car and ran toward the stairs, stopped for a moment at the bottom of the steps leading up to the footbridge, extended the middle fingers on both her hands, and flipped off Tommy. Then she ran up the steps to the bridge and into his arms. They kissed passionately for a full minute or so and then walked back down to where Lew was waiting with the lunch.

"I want to say this to you, Jamie Lynn, and I want to say it to you and your dad, too. I've been an idiot, only thinking of myself. I love you, Jamie Lynn, I've always loved you. I admire, appreciate, and love that you are saving yourself for me and for our marriage. Your dad taught me those words."

Jamie started laughing.

"I promise you I won't make an issue of this ever again," Tommy continued. "The short time we were apart, I realized what it would be like to lose you, and I can't ever let that happen again." He turned to her father. "So, Lew, I have to ask you this. I'm in love with your daughter, and I want to marry her. May I have your blessing on that?

"Yes, Tommy," Lew said. "You have my blessing to marry my daughter."

Chapter 8

Finding Abby

Jamie left Pueblo and drove to Colorado Springs on his temporary fire watch assignment. He exited the freeway at Cimarron to head up Highway 24 but decided to stop for gas and coffee at Benny's Convenience Store on Eighth Street.

As usual, Benny would not charge him for the coffee, and Jamie went through his usual obligatory complaining about Benny's always giving him the free coffee. It was, as always, to no avail.

The next thing Jamie knew, he was on the floor, and he was having trouble breathing. Benny had him by his left arm, and a young red-haired girl was holding his right arm. She was crying. "I think you're my dad," he remembered her saying.

They managed to get him to his feet, and Benny gave him some water. "Let me take you over to the dining area, Jamie," he said.

He helped him into a booth and table, and Jamie sat down. The girl sat down across from him and took his hands in hers.

When he regained his composure, he asked her, "What is your mother's name, miss?"

"Abby, her name is Abby, sir," Jamie Lynn said.

"I knew it. I knew it the very minute I saw you. You look just like she used to look, I mean, identical, spitting image." Tears filled his eyes, and he couldn't speak for a few minutes.

"I have to find her," he finally said. "I've been looking for her for fourteen years."

"What happened to you?" the girl said." Mom waited for months. But they stopped searching, and told her you were dead. She lost it, really bad."

"I was in an accident. My truck was knocked off the road by a rock slide. I hit my head and couldn't remember anything for a long time. This sweet old woman, a hermit type, rescued me and took me in. She took care of me for six months. Finally, I was found by some other park rangers, but It was two years before I really got back to normal. When were you born, Jamie?"

"I was born November twenty-fourth of eighty-six."

"So, Abby was pregnant with you the last time I saw her. God, what I would give to have seen you grow up. My goodness, you look so much like your mother. Your mother—your mom, where's your mom now? Is Abby still alive? Please tell me Abby is still alive."

"Yes, she's still alive, we live in The Springs. My mom is a nurse. She works at Eisenhower Hospital. Mom was married to my stepdad. They're divorced now, but he still lives in The Springs. He's a good man, the best dad any kid could ever want. He loves me like I'm his own kid."

"So, you knew about me?"

"Oh, yes. My mom told me about you when I was very young. I call Lew, that's my daddy, Daddy because he's the only dad I've ever known. I don't really know what to call you. Should I call you—can I call you Dad?"

"It would bring me back to life if you did that," he said.

"Every time my mom sees a park services vehicle, she starts crying."

"And she named you Jamie, after me? That's just awesome. What is your full name?"

"My middle name is Lynn, I go by Jamie Lynn."

Jamie smiled. "That's my mother's middle name," he said. "I'm going to have to take you home. They *have* to see you. They will go insane over you."

"I'd like that, but now we have to figure out now how to tell my mom about you."

"I know, how do we do this?"

"Well, I can't just walk in the door with you. That would freak her out. I'll have to call her first."

"Is she at home now?"

"I think so. Why don't I call her? Are you ready for this?"

"I don't know," he said. "I've thought about this moment, run it over in my mind a thousand times, but there was never a daughter in my calculations. God, Jamie Lynn, it's just so wonderful to find out about you. You're just more than I could ever have imagined or hoped for."

"And you're everything Mom said you were. your smile, it's everything my mom described. I mean, I've seen pictures, but she was right—they don't do you justice, you're cool, you're— you're my father. I'm still processing that. I'm so glad you're still alive." She stood up, went to his side of the table, and hugged him around his neck. When she let him go, Jamie was crying again.

He held up his hand to signal her to wait a moment. Then he said, "Your mom may not believe you at first. See what she says and let me talk to her if she agrees to talk to me."

Jamie Lynn nodded and started dialing Abby's cell phone.

"Hello, honey," Abby said. "Where are you."

"Mom, are you at home?"

"No, I'm just leaving work. Where are you?"

"I'm at the convenience store at Eighth and Cimarron. I was going to Garden of the Gods to meet some friends, and I stopped to get gas."

"What's going on, honey? You sound strange."

"Mom are you driving yet?"

"I'm just leaving the parking lot, why?"

"Don't leave. Pull into a parking space and turn off the engine. I have something to tell you."

"Now you're scaring me. Jamie Lynn, are you okay?

"Yes, Mom, I'm very okay, but I have something I have to tell you that you won't believe at first, but I have to make you believe it."

"Jamie Lynn, stop playing games and tell me what you're talking about."

"Mom, Jamie—as in Jamie Cain, my father—is alive, and I'm sitting here looking at him, right now."

"All right, Jamie Lynn, I need you to listen to me and listen closely. I don't know who that man is that you are with, but don't you dare get in a car with him. Where are you again?"

"Mom, I'm at Benny's Convenience Store at the corner of Eighth and Cimarron."

Abby immediately hung up, and dialed nine-one-one. She reported the incident and asked them to send the police to check on her daughter. Then she called Jamie Lynn back. "Don't leave with him, Jamie Lynn. You go to your car and get the hell out of there, right now."

"He's alive, Mom, I'm telling you the truth, it's him.

My father, Jamie Cain is alive. I've seen his ID."

Abby was in near panic now. "Jamie Lynn, some-body could have forged that ID card and that man might just be someone who looks like Jamie and is trying to lure you into going with them. Oh God, don't get in the car with that man." She heard a man's voice talking to Jamie Lynn.

Then a man spoke on Jamie Lynn's phone. "Abby," he said. "I completely understand your concern. Do this, call nine-one-one and tell them that your daughter is talk-ing to a man who claims to be her dead father. Tell them you're concerned and ask them if they'll send a unit to make sure your daughter's safe."

"Okay. I'm going to come there, too. Will you wait there until I get there?"

"Yes, Abby, I will wait here. I've been looking for you for fourteen years. I can wait until you get here."

"What did she say?" Jamie Lynn asked when he hung up.

"She's coming here."

"Did she say she was going to call nine-one-one like you said?"

"She already called."

"Really, how do you know that?"

"Because she calmed down suddenly."

Abby buried her face in her hands and broke down. She didn't know if this was a dream come true or her worst nightmare. "Oh God," she prayed out loud, "don't let anyone hurt my baby."

She drove toward I-25, still praying as she went. She called the police again, while she was driving and asked if they had sent someone to check on her daughter. The operator told her she was going to patch her through to the officer who answered the call and was at the scene as they were speaking. Abby breathed a sigh of relief when she heard the man's voice on her phone.

"This is Officer Simmons, who am I speaking to?"

"I'm Abby Morgan, I asked them to have someone go there and make sure my daughter is safe."

"Oh, yes, ma'am, Mrs. Morgan, your daughter is fine. The man she is with is the park ranger who was missing for six months in the wilderness, back in 1986 and was finally rescued. They're here waiting for you. I'll wait here until you arrive."

"Oh, thank God, and thank you, Officer, I'm not too far away." She drove the rest of the way in a virtual mental fog, not fully absorbing what was happening to her. She took the Cimarron exit, turned west, went to Eighth Street, and turned right, still not sure what she would find when she got to the store.

Her mind was racing ahead of her, and her heart was almost beating out of her chest.

"There's the police car," she said to herself. A park services truck was sitting in a space on the left side of the store." "Okay, I'm feeling a little better about this."

She saw Jamie Lynn standing outside the front door of the store. She had her arms wrapped around a man, and her head was resting on his chest. His left arm was around her shoulder.

"He looks like Jamie," she said out loud. "My God, he looks like Jamie."

She got out of her car and started walking toward the two of them, still crying almost uncontrollably. When she reached Jamie, she collapsed into his arms, and he held her up to keep her from falling.

"Oh , J—Jamie, I'm s—sorry, I'm so sorry, I'm so s—orry," she stammered." She continued crying and telling him she was sorry over and over again.

He took her face in his hands and looked at her, lovingly, adoringly. "Abby, Abby, why are you sorry? You have nothing to be sorry for."

"I should have waited for you. I'm sorry. My life was over when they told me you were dead. I wanted to die too, but I was carrying your baby. I'm so sorry."

"Stop saying you're sorry, Abby. I was lost six months, and I had injuries. I had amnesia. I didn't remember you for two years. It's a long story, but we have time now. I'll tell you all about it when this all soaks in. I'm still numb from finding out I have a daughter, and she's a Xerox copy of you. I've been living in fear all this time that you might not even be alive. Now I find that you're alive and I have a daughter. What a gift she must have been to you."

"She's blessed my life so much," Abby said through her tears, "You can't imagine."

"Yeah, I can," Jamie said. "We have a lot to talk about, Abby. Where do we go from here?"

"Let's go to my house," Abby said. "We do have a lot to talk about. Do you know where Westmoreland Road is?

"I'm not from The Springs," Jamie said.

"Just follow me, I'll drive slow."

♥♥♥

Abby made coffee, and the three of them sat at her dining room table talking. Jamie's eyes kept alternating between Abby and Jamie Lynn. His face beamed.

"I'd almost forgotten that smile," Abby said, reaching out to touch his face with her hand.

"I haven't smiled this much in the last fourteen years," he said. "I'd given up hope, and then right out of the blue, here you are, and with a bonus." He nodded toward Jamie Lynn. "Why did you decide to name her Jamie Lynn?"

"I'd planned to name her after you from the very beginning. You were named after your mother, so I thought it would be appropriate to name your son or daughter after you. I knew it would be confusing when I started telling her about you, you both having the same name, so I gave her your mother's middle name."

"Well, I'm honored. Did she tell you, no she couldn't have yet, but one of her friends called out her name in the store, and we both answered him? Then we just looked at each other, dumbfounded."

"That must have been some experience for the two of you, in that store."

"It was a miracle from heaven," Jamie said. "How can I interpret it as anything else? The daughter I didn't even know I had, just happened to show up in the exact same convenience store where I stop for coffee and gas all the time. All the convenience stores in this city, and she just happened to walk into the one I'm in. Omygosh, I'm channeling Humphry Bogart in Casablanca."

Abby laughed. "I was about to say that. But I was panic stricken, I mean you have no idea how scared I was when she called me."

"I know you were. We thought for a while about how to contact you. Jamie—uh, Jamie Lynn —knew we couldn't just come find you because that would freak you out."

"Yeah, that would have been too much all at once," Abby said.

"He knew you had already called the cops before he told you to call them," Jamie Lynn said.

"You did? How did you know?"

"You're a mother, for one thing, and also, there was a disconnect in your conversation with Jamie Lynn, and when you called her back, you were calm and agreeable and asked me if I would be here when you got here. The police showed up about a minute after I told Jamie Lynn that you had already called them. I figured you had hung up and called nine-one-one."

Abby smiled. "You're right, that's exactly what I did."

"I want to take you two to my folks. They have to know you're okay and they have to meet her." He nodded again toward Jamie Lynn. "And I'd like to show you my cabin." He appeared to be in thought for a moment. "Wait, Abby, am I being too presumptuous? How foolish of me to assume that you don't have someone—"

"I don't have a boyfriend, Jamie, if that's what you're asking."

"A man," he said. "You're still just as beautiful as you ever were, you must have—"

"There's no one, Jamie. Lew and I divorced two years ago. We parted as friends, and he still has a very close relationship with Jamie Lynn. He loves her very much. I am thankful for that."

"She told me that, and I am too—thankful, I mean— that she had someone like that." He pushed his chair back and stood up.

"Will you stand up, Abby?" he asked her. She did as he asked, and he wrapped both arms around her and hugged her. He started weeping, and his body shook.

"I'm so happy to find you alive and well," he finally managed to tell her.

"If I had only waited another two months," Abby said, "our lives would have been so different. I'm so sorry, Jamie."

He motioned for Jamie Lynn to come around the table to where he and Abby were standing. They each raised an arm and included her in the hug. Abby was crying too, now.

"Jamie Lynn," Jamie said.

"Yes, Dad," she responded.

"Please tell your mom to stop apologizing to me."

They all started laughing. Jamie took Abby's face in both his hands and looked at her in the same loving way he had at the store. "Abby," he said, "just on the outside chance that you don't realize it yet, I'm still in love with you. I'll never stop loving you."

"I still love you too, Jamie," she said.

"Tommy's here," Jamie Lynn shouted and ran to the front door.

Jamie looked at Abby.

"Tommy is Jamie Lynn's boyfriend," Abby said, "since they were eight years old. They're going to get married eventually. You have to meet him."

Jamie Lynn came in leading a young man by the hand. He was wearing army fatigues and was about the same height as Jamie. "Come on, Tommy, I want you to meet someone. This is Jamie Cain, my Dad."

Jamie shook hands with Tommy. He was a handsome boy, rugged and muscular, with dark hair and eyes and olive skin, and he carried himself well. Tommy had a look of total confusion on his face. "I thought you were dead," he said.

"I was," Jamie said, "but I came back to life."

The comment provided no help to Tommy, who was still trying to sort things out.

"We just found him today, Tommy," Jamie Lynn said. "He wasn't really dead. He was rescued, and he's been looking for Mom all this time."

"Well, I'm glad to meet you, sir. I'm Tommy Baker, and I've heard a lot about you."

"Well, this is the first I've heard of you, so I'm sorry to say I haven't heard anything about you. I didn't even know I had a daughter until today."

"Tommy won a Bronze Star in Afghanistan," Jamie Lynn said.

"That's fantastic, Tommy. Good for you. Are you stationed at Carson now?"

"I am. I'll get out of the service in two-thousand-six. Jamie Lynn and I are going to get married."

"Well, you look like a perfect couple to me."

"Mom, Tommy is going to take me to Daddy's. Can I go now?"

"Of course, honey," Abby said, "Don't forget your bag."

"I won't," she said and ran to her room. She came out in an instant with her clothes bag, ran up to Jamie, and threw her arms around him. "I'm so glad you found us, Dad, I love you. I'll be back Sunday night. Why don't you take Mom to see your cabin?"

"I love you, too, darling, and I'm glad I found you, too."

"She spends one weekend a month with Lew. He's very busy, and she's always busy, or she'd probably go more often. They have a really good relationship."

"I would never try and get in the way of that, Abby. That's a gift from God. I'm glad she had someone. It just breaks my heart that I was not there to see her grow up."

"I know. Over the years, as I watched it all play out, I always secretly wished it were you who was here with us."

"I'm not going to ask you what happened with your marriage to Lew, and I'm not going to say I'm glad you broke up. I just want to know you again, know the girl, know the woman, I fell in love with. If you decide that you can be my love again, then every promise I ever made you is still good. For me, nothing has changed since we met in the hall by our lockers in high school."

"And I want to know what has happened to *you* since I lost you," Abby said. "And I want to tell you all about my life since then, as well. It will take some time, but I want to do it. Let's go to your cabin for the weekend if you want to."

"I called my chief, when we were driving to your house, and told him what happened. I'll have to drop the company truck off at the office and get mine but, yes, I'd like for you to see my cabin. It's a really nice place."

e⁄ɔe⁄ɔ

"You finally got a new truck, I see," Abby said, as they changed vehicles at the park service station.

"I ran the wheels off the old one. I bought this one a few years ago. I don't put a lot of miles on it. I've turned into a home body."

"Where did you get this?" Abby asked, looking at the poem on the wall in his cabin.

"The poem? I got that in a little arts and crafts place in Manitou Springs."

She read the poem to herself.

In dreams, she comes to visit me
in misty clouds of finery
on wings of efflorescent skies
through twilight hazed myopic eyes
from far away and long ago
a winsome girl I used to know
In dreams, we walk through verdant leas
my thoughts unclear, escaping me
And from my mind and from my heart
the 'dreams once dreamed' will not depart
For this heart, I've guarded jealously
I find does not belong to me
Yet still is hers, I loved her so
tho' far away and long ago
this girl I used to know

A tear ran down her cheek as she rubbed the spot where Jamie had written her name.

"It's beautiful," she said.

"I started dreaming about you. You see, after I was rescued, I had amnesia. I didn't even know my folks for a while. But, eventually, my doctor took me home, and that triggered something in my mind. And I remembered them.

"That must have been hard for your mom and dad."

"Especially my mom, it was. There was this sweet old woman, named Ona Mabry. Ona was born a hundred years too late. She lived alone, in the wilderness, after her husband died. Ona found me and took me to her home and took care of me for months. When I got better, I got out and started shooting deer for her to stock her smoke house. That's how the park rangers found me. They were going to arrest me, but one of them recognized me. My mom met Ona and hugged her like she was her grandmother. That surprised the hell out of Ona because, honestly, she didn't smell all that sweet."

"What happened to Ona?" Abby asked him.

"Ona died," Jamie said. "She made one of her rare trips into Leadville and had a heart attack in the post office. By the time I found out about it, the state had already cremated her."

Abby sensed that Jamie was saddened just by talking about the woman.

He covered it up by merging right back into his previous line of conversion. "And what was even stranger was that I had pictures of you all over my room, but I didn't know who you were. When I got an apartment in Lakewood, I went home to get all my stuff, and I took your pictures down and brought them with me and put them on the walls of my apartment, and I still didn't know who you were.

"Then I started having these dreams. I would be walking on grassy hills, there were snow-capped mountains off in the distance, but it was warm. A woman was walking away from me, sort of looking back at me, but I couldn't see her face. She was walking, and I was running, but I couldn't catch her. I didn't have the dreams every night, just every so often, but it was always the same. Then one day I was in The Springs, and I went to Manitou Springs just killing time, and I found that poem. I bought it and put it on my wall because of the dreams. The very next night I was back at my apartment, I had the dream again, but, this time, I could see the woman's face, and it was the woman in the picture on my wall."

"This is sending chills up my spine," Abby said.

"Yeah, mine too. So, I called my mother and asked who the girl was in the picture. She was kind of afraid to tell me, at first, but I insisted, so she said, 'the girl's name is Abby.' Then I wrote your name on the poem. My dad came over to check on me and asked me about the picture, and I told him I had to find you. That was in 'eighty-eight. So, I've been looking for you for fourteen years."

"Did you not meet any women in all that time? I mean, you were a healthy, normal male animal, very healthy if I recall correctly. You had to have—"

"I came close several times but only went all the way once, that was about four or five years ago."

"What happened?"

"Basically, she told that I was emotionally unavailable."

"Really?" Abby said, chuckling. "So, you were just a one-night stand?"

"I discovered that the only way I could have sex with the woman was to pretend she was you. That woman thought I was in love with her. She showed up at my cabin a few days later, ready to move in and begin what she thought was going to be a long-term relationship. I had to tell her that she misread my signals and my emotions. I had to tell her that I was searching for my lost love and the passion I showed her was intended for that woman and not for her."

"We've been living parallel lives, my love," Abby said. "The last thing Lew said to me, before he asked me for a divorce, was that he had to find someone who wasn't in love with a dead man."

"Wow, I don't know what to say about that, Abby."

"There isn't much to say. For the most part, we had a good marriage. Lew is a great dad. He practically worships Jamie Lynn. But our marriage was based on co-dependency from the very beginning."

"How so?"

"He was a professor at a college in Colby, Kansas. That's where my mother and I went to stay with my Aunt Betty when we left Golden. Lew was giving a grief seminar. He had lost his wife to cancer three years before, and he was not over her and didn't believe he would ever get over her completely. He knew how I felt about you. We became friends, and he asked me to marry him, promising to take care of me and the baby. He's a decent man, and I said yes. It was part of my healing process, I suppose."

"You don't have to explain to me why you went on living, Abby," Jamie said. "I expect to meet him eventually. Lew sounds like a great guy. He loved you, and he loves Jamie Lynn. What else do I need to know about him."

"He paid for me to go to nursing school so I could support myself and Jamie Lynn, and he gave me the house when we divorced. It's almost paid off now."

"You'd better stop this," Jamie said, "or I might be forced to talk you into going back to him."

"Oh, God, Jamie, it's like dream, seeing you again after all this time. There were times I just wanted to die. I think I would have died of a broken heart if it were not for Jamie Lynn."

"Searching for you is the only thing that has kept me alive. It's the craziest thing but, every time I came through The Springs, I could feel your presence. I mean I

felt like you were there. I don't know why, maybe because I knew you went to school here, Mitchell High
School, by the way."

"Oh, how did you find that out?" she asked.

"It took me months, getting the fax numbers or email
addresses of every high school in the Colorado Springs
school district. A lady at the office sent letters to every
one of them. Mitchell came back with info on you. They
told me you had relocated to Golden High School in
1984. Well, no shit, I wanted to tell them. I already knew
that."

Abby chuckled. "We moved to The Springs in nine-
ty-three."

"Why didn't you ever go see my folks?"

"I wanted to," she said. "I started to a dozen times,
but I felt so terrible about leaving without letting them
know where I was going. I was a mess. You wouldn't
have known me at that time. When I found out I was
pregnant, my mother wanted me to get an abortion. I told
her to go to hell, then she wanted me to hit your folks up
for money."

"You should have."

"No, I shouldn't have, Jamie. I didn't want them to
know we were sleeping together before we were married."

Jamie laughed. "My mom and dad were sleeping together before *they* were married. I wish you had gone to
them. They would have taken care of you and the baby.

You could have lived in the guest house, or in my room, for as long as you wanted or needed to, forever."

"I wish that too, now. That's just one more thing I'm sorry for. I made so many mistakes. When Lew asked me to marry him, it seemed like the most logical way to get on with my life."

"That wasn't a mistake, Abby. From what you've told me, I think that was the best thing you could have done for both you and for Jamie Lynn. I just need you back in my life now."

From the dining room table, where they were sitting, Abby could see into Jamie's room. She pointed in that direction. "Is that the same bed you did that woman in?"

"Yes," he said, nodding, "but I've washed the sheets since then."

Abby stood up from her chair and walked into the bedroom. She turned back the bedcovers and began to unbutton her blouse. Jamie watched her as she removed her pants and bra. She got into the bed, pulled the covers up to her neck, and stared at him

Still sitting at the dining room table, Jamie felt his breathing and heartbeat accelerate. He stood up, walked over next to her, and sat down on the side of the bed. He took her hand in his and kissed it several times, very tenderly.

"I've had this dream before," he said. "I usually wake up before I get my shoes off."

She smiled at him. "Then start with the shirt and

work your way down," she said. "Leave the shoes on if you must."

When his last shoe was on the floor with the rest of his clothes, Abby pulled back the covers, and he slid in beside her. He put his arm under her neck and caressed her face with his free hand and fingers. He kissed her, softly, as if he was savoring her lips. He remembered that, when they had been lovers in their early years, there was nothing in the world like Abby's lips. Placing his lips on Abby's always made him dizzy. It was happening again now. After fourteen years without her, nothing had changed.

"Abby, I missed you so much," he said, as their kisses became more desperate. Jamie kept reminding himself that it was not a dream this time. He was really with Abby, and they were making love, just like all the times he'd dreamed about it over the years, but this time it was real.

"My love, my love," she whispered and then said it over and over.

Later, he held her in his arms as they lay there, caressing each other, contemplating the beauty of the marvelous thing that had just happened between them.

"I'm sorry, Abby," he said, finally.

"What in the world for?" she asked.

"For having an accident, getting amnesia and disappearing for six months."

She laughed and slapped him across the chest. "I forgive you," she said. "Just don't let it happen again."

"I want to dance with you," he said.

"Where do you want to go?"

"The living room."

She laughed. "Well, I don't think we'll have any trouble getting a table.

He got out of bed and put on his undershorts and turned on the radio to a country and western station. Abby got up and put on her panties and bra.

"The sign on the door said casual dress," she said.

"You're a little overdressed, but it's okay," he replied.

"Do you come here often?"

"Never been here before," he said.

"Couldn't get a date?" she said, smiling at him mischievously.

He kissed her. "I've been waiting for the right girl to come along."

"How long would you have waited, Jamie," Abby asked him, suddenly more serious.

"I was prepared to meet you one day when we both showed up in the same nursing home."

She burst out laughing. "Oh my, you really have not changed a bit."

"Nothing has changed, Abby," he said, "except we're not in high school anymore. Shouldn't we get on with the plans we had after we got out of high school?"

"Do you still want to marry me, Jamie?"

"You're the love of my life, Abby."

"All you have to do is ask me," she said.

He took both her hands in his. "Will you marry me, Abby?"

"Yes, Jamie, I will marry you. I was starting to wonder if you were ever going to ask me."

"Well, I sort of got sidetracked, but now I've figured out what I want to be when I grow up."

"Oh, well, after what you just did to me in bed a while ago, I can assure you, sir, you are as grown up as you are ever going to get."

"So, is that a yes?" he said.

"It's a yes, but I don't need a big affair, Jamie. A justice of the peace will be fine with me. Your daughter is going to marry that soldier not long after she graduates from high school, sound familiar? I want to have a big wedding for them. For us, I just want to be your wife like I was going to be sixteen years ago."

"Then let's do it soon, I want to take you both to see my folks. They'll be thrilled."

"I'm a little nervous to see your mom and dad."

"I wish you wouldn't be," he said. "They're not judgmental people. They'll understand what you did, Abby."

"But I kept your daughter away from them. I tried a dozen times to take her to see them, but I felt so ashamed. Had I done that years ago, things would have been so different. I don't deserve their forgiveness, but I do hope they understand."

"I know my folks, Abby. They'll still love you just like I do."

❦❦❦

He was awake before dawn the next morning, gently shaking her in an attempt to wake her up. "Abby."

"Hmm?"

"You awake?"

"I am now."

"I'm making coffee. you have to see the sun come up over the mountains."

"What time is it, Jamie?"

"Before dawn, come on."

"Where to?"

"The front deck," he said. "I'll bring the coffee. Cream, right?

"Cream."

"Grab the blanket, it's a little cool out this early in the morning."

Picking up the blanket at the foot of the bed, she wrapped it around her and walked out onto the front deck of his cabin.

He'd turned on the porch light so she could find her way to the table and chairs. He was there quickly with a tray on which sat two cups, a cup of cream, and a decanter of coffee like they brought to your table at some restaurants.

"Here," he said, tossing her a pair of knee-high wool socks, "in case your feet get cold."

"The coffee is good," she said, as she put the socks on her feet.

"I do this, every morning I'm here."

"You're gone a lot?"

"Occasionally, they send me to assist other stations, and if it's overnight, we stay in motels. Once they sent me up to the Denver area, and I went home and stayed with my folks. Most of the time, though, I'm here at the cabin."

"It's a beautiful place, Jamie, it looks like you," she mused.

"I usually bring the poem or a picture of you out here with me and sit here and feel sorry for myself."

"Oh, my gosh, I never know if you're serious or joking with me."

"I'm serious," he said. "I really do that."

"Well, now you have the real thing."

He smiled and nodded. "The sun is starting to come up," he said.

"Wow, it's beautiful. I remember when I was in school, I would be up early enough to see the sun hit Pikes Peak in the morning. It was so awesome. I haven't done that in years. I'm always at the hospital, working, or sleeping late after working the night shift, and I just don't take the time to do it anymore."

"We need to do that for you again."

"Where are we going to live, Jamie, when we get married, I mean?" The look on his face told her that it had not even crossed his mind.

"I've been in a dream world since I found you. I hadn't thought about the logistics of this thing. I don't know. I can't move into another man's house."

"Of course, you can, Jamie," Abby said. "It's not another man's house, it's my house. It wasn't paid for when Lew and I divorced. Granted, it was very generous of him to sign it over to me, but I've been making double payments on it since then. I plan to pay it off as quickly as I can. It's my house, darling. I still have to work, and Jamie Lynn goes to school. You can drive to Pueblo to work, can't you?"

"Yes, I can. Are you sure that won't be inappropriate? I want to be with you and Jamie Lynn."

"Then 'be' with us. With us is where you belong."

"How much do you owe on the house?"

"I don't know exactly, maybe fifteen thousand or so, why?

"Why don't we pay it off?" he said.

"I don't understand," Abby said. "I don't have enough money. That's why I've been making double payments, to get it paid off faster."

"I can pay it off," he said.

"I can't ask you to do that?"

"You don't have to ask, Abby, I want to do it. If it will make things easier for you, I want to do it."

"You'll make things easier just by being there with me."

"Abby," he said and took her hands in his, across the table. "I don't drink, I don't do drugs, I don't chase women. I've worked and saved my money, hoping I'd find you one day, and now I have. I have a virtual 'piss pot' full of money in the bank, and there is nothing I'd rather do than spend it on you and Jamie Lynn."

"And a piss pot full of money is a substantial amount, if I recall correctly."

"Let me do this, Abby, please. Get your pay-off balance, and I'll write you a check."

"Okay, Jamie, as soon as we're married, and you move into the house."

"Oh, so now you want to hold me to a pre-nup?"

Laughing, she said, "If that's what it takes, my love."

"It's a deal," he said. "Now, I'm going to call my mom and tell her about you and Jamie Lynn, okay?"

"Yes, it's okay, we've kept it from them long enough."

ে৲৩৶৩

"Hello," the voice on the phone said. It was Will Cain, Jamie's dad.

"Hey, Pop, I forgot you had caller ID," Jamie said. "That threw me off for a minute. Is Mom at home."

"She is, she's in the living room here next to me. What's up, Jamie?"

"I have something to tell you both. Can you put the phone on speaker?"

"Okay," Will said, "it's on speaker."

"I'm coming to see you next weekend." He looked at Abby and mouthed the word "Okay?"

Abby nodded.

"I have some good news to tell you, Mom."

"You're being transferred to Denver so you'll be back at home with us?"

"No, even better than that," he said.

"Now what in the world could be better than you coming back home for good?"

"It's the best thing that's ever happened to me in my life, Mom."

There was silence for a moment then his mother gasped. "Oh, my God, Jamie, do you mean..."

"Yes, Mom, the *very* best thing."

"Oh, Jamie, you've found Abby. Oh, thank God. How is she?"

"She's perfect, Mom, but that's only half of it. You have a sixteen-year-old granddaughter named Jamie Lynn. I'm sure if you look hard enough you can find something in her that looks like me but basically, she's a clone of Abby. I mean she looks just like her. It's a long story. I'll tell you when we get there."

"Oh, I'm so happy for you, and for Abby. Okay, son, tell them both we love them very much."

"Well, there you go, Abby," he said after he hung up the phone. "Now we just have to work out all the details. I love you, Abby, I want to make things easier for you, not more complicated. So just figure out how we should proceed, and I'll follow your lead."

⌘⌘⌘

"So, we're going to meet my grandparents?" Jamie Lynn said excitedly.

"We are darling," Abby said, "and you'll love them, believe me. They are truly great people."

Jamie drove them through Golden on the way to his folks' house in Coal Creek Canyon. "This is Golden High School, Jamie Lynn," Jamie said. "It was right in that school where your mother and I first met."

"I've heard this story, Dad, you told her, um—what was it he told you, Mom?"

"He said, as I was getting ready to leave my locker, 'hold up there a minute, precious, where did you come from,' or something like that. Then he said, 'you can't just waltz in here and take my breath away, then leave me wondering if I dreamed you up or if you really happened.' I think that's what he said."

"Yeah, it was something like that, and then I asked you to go get a burger and a coke with me after school. It was love at first sight."

"That is *soo* romantic, so it really happens?"

"Yes, Jamie Lynn, it really happens," Abby answered. "It happened to your dad and me that very first day we met. It was pure magic."

"I think it happened with me and Tommy too, I mean he did come back after he broke up with me that time."

"He came back begging you to forgive him, didn't he?" Abby said.

"Yes, he did, just like you said he would."

෴

Jamie's folks were outside in the front yard when they pulled up in the driveway. Jamie's Mom ran to Abby first and hugged her tenderly. "Thank God you finally came home," she said. Both women were crying. After a couple of minutes, she let go of Abbie and, still crying, said, "I have to see my granddaughter."

Jamie Lynn came walking toward her.

"Oh my God, I'm looking at your mother eighteen years ago. You're so beautiful, darling, let me hug you."

After all the hugging was done, they all went into the house, and Will spoke. "It was confusing enough with two Jamies in the family, and now we have three. I guess we're going to have to set some ground rules," he said. "Okay, my wife is Grandma Jamie, and you, sweetheart, he pointed at Jamie Lynn, "are Jamie Lynn, or granddaughter, and my son is Jamie. Everybody okay with that?" Everyone clapped their approval.

Abby motioned to Mrs. Cain. "Can we talk in private? There are some things I need to explain to you, if you don't mind."

"Not at all, honey. I'll make Will and the other Jamies go out on the patio."

"We sit out here almost every morning, Granddaughter, and watch the sun come up on the Front Range and then watch it go down at night," Will said. "It's really beautiful, you'll see this evening."

"I'm looking forward to it, uh—what do I call you?"

"My other grandkids call me Grandpa. I'd be honored if you choose to do the same."

"Okay, Grandpa, I want to watch the sun go down on the Front Range with you tonight."

"We're going to have to have a get together. Jamie, invite your sister and Evan and their two girls. My God, I'll be floating in a sea of estrogen with all the women in the house."

"Mom and Dad are going to get married, Grandpa. Maybe they can do it here."

"I think that's a great idea, Jamie Lynn. What do you think, son?"

"I think Abby would love it. She doesn't want a big affair, and this would be perfect. I'll talk to her about it after she and Mom are finished talking."

"What are they talking about, son," Will asked.

"Abby wanted to explain to Mom why she left without contacting you guys and why she never brought Jamie Lynn around to meet you. She went through a pretty bad time when I disappeared."

"We all did, son, it was a terrible time for all of us."

☙☙☙

Two weeks later, Jamie, Abby, and Jamie Lynn returned to the Cain home for their wedding. Will had acquired a local pastor to perform the service and had made all the arrangements.

It was to be a family affair with no friends or acquaintances invited. Jamie's sister, Clare, and brother-in-law, Evan Garner, were there with their two girls, now eighteen and nineteen. Evan, being Jamie's best friend would act as his best man. Jamie Lynn would be her mom's maid of honor.

It was a simple ceremony. Jamie made a stammering attempt at professing his undying love for Abby, but everyone got his point. Before the preacher pronounced them husband and wife, Abby made an announcement.

"I want to read a poem," she said. "Jamie has a poem that brought him some comfort while he was looking for me, and I have a poem that, I won't say it brought me comfort but it does pretty much sum up my life during the time I had to live without him. I wrote this during the lowest part of my life, after Jamie was given up for dead."

Jamie Lynn handed her a folded piece of paper. Abby unfolded it and started to read. Her voice trembled a bit and Jamie took her hand.

"It's okay, baby," he said, "go on."

"The poem is called, Day's End," Abby said.

"'Day's End
It is the end of day
It is the end of all my days
for now, you are gone
the one I could not lose
And lo! The earth continues
as if it hasn't noticed
Arise! Arise oh brazen Sun
(Thou damned officious star)
Thy presence is offensive now
But God ordains you should
Tho' life and time refuse to pause
as I thought they surely would
But when my journey is complete
I'll join you by and by
somewhere up in Coal Creek Canyon
where the mountains meet the sky
So yet these many years I wait
for the clock to strike again
growing old and gray, alone
just waiting for Day's end.'"

Abby was crying by the time she finished reading, and everyone on the patio was stunned into silence.

The preacher was the first to speak. "With the power vested in me by the State of Colorado, I now pronounce you husband and wife. You may kiss your wife now."

"I think I'm just going to hold her in my arms for a while," Jamie said.

Chapter 9

The Wedding

2004:

With both her dads' encouragement, Jamie Lynn agreed to attend UCCS to pursue a nursing degree like her mother had done.

"If you're going to marry Tommy Baker," Lew advised her, "you need to be prepared to support yourself. If he decides to stay in the army, he'll never make enough money to support you very well."

"He's not going to make a career out of the army, Daddy," Jamie Lynn said.

"Then what does he intend to do for a living, honey?"

"I don't know, but he'll find a job."

"Tommy didn't even graduate from high school, Jamie Lynn. What kind of job can he get that pays more than minimum wage?"

"He got his GED in the army, and he is smarter than you give him credit for."

"He still has two years left in the service, so he'd better be thinking about what he's going to do for a living. Where are you going to live when you get married?"

"We're going to live with Tommy's mother," she said.

"Does Tommy's mother know this?"

"She wants us to. She's really happy about it."

"Well, I'm really glad that Jamie was with me on talking you into going to college."

"Yeah, nothing like having my two dads conspiring against me."

"Oh, come on, Jamie Lynn, you know we both want what's best for you."

"I know, Daddy, I was just joking. I love you both. You're both too good to me."

"So, Jamie is good to you?"

"Are you kidding? He treats me like I'm a princess. He does anything I ask him to do and looks for things to do for me. He's wonderful. Oh, I'm sorry, Daddy, I didn't mean to—"

"It's okay, darling," Lew said. "He *is* your father and he missed out on being with you all those years. I can't blame him for treating you like you're the only daughter in the world—for him, you are. You are for me, too, for that matter. How is he with your mom?"

"Oh my God, they practically worship each other. He never takes his eyes off her, except to talk to me, I mean. He really loves her. I guess they really were in love before they got separated."

"Okay, Jamie Lynn, I get the message, I had to ask, didn't I?"

"I'm sorry, Daddy," she said.

"No, it's all right, honey. I'm glad you're both happy.

"Don't you ever go out, Daddy?" she asked him.

"Well, it interesting that you should mention that. I have been dating a woman from school. I'm thinking maybe that you could go to dinner with us tonight."

"What's her name?"

"Her name is Megyn, and she teaches English Lit."

"Are you going to marry her?"

"I don't know," he said. "We've only been dating a couple of months. We'll have to wait and see."

"Wow," Jamie Lynn said when Megyn walked out of her apartment. "She's pretty flashy, Daddy. I hope you have enough Viagra."

"Jamie Lynn!" Lew said, just a bit disconcerted. "You're a little more worldly than I'm ready for. Please confine your comments to more genteel conversation, if you don't mind."

"Okay, Daddy, but I have to say I am impressed."

Megyn had perfectly coiffed shoulder -length blonde hair and striking blue eyes. She was well built and the black strapless dress she was wearing fit her like it was designed for her and for her alone. She carried herself with extreme confidence. "Wow," Lew said when she got into the car. "Why don't you dress like that at school?"

"They don't pay me enough," she said.

"Megyn, this is my daughter, Jamie Lynn, in the back seat."

"Hi, Megyn," Jamie Lynn said.

"Hello, Jamie Lynn," Megyn replied coldly. "Where are we going, Lew?"

"How does the Pepper Tree sound?" he said.

"I've never been there but I've heard it's really good," Megyn said.

"How about you, Jamie Lynn. You trust your daddy to pick a restaurant?"

"Well, of course, Daddy," she replied.

ℰ✴ℰ✴

"Wow," Jamie Lynn said, "this is really expensive."

"Now, come on, honey, this is a special occasion. I wanted you and Megyn to meet, and I didn't want to skimp on dinner. Let's enjoy ourselves, okay?"

Megyn smiled. "You're the boss, Lew," she said. "That's why I'm so crazy about you."

Jamie Lynn looked surprised at Megyn and then at Lew."

"Megyn and I are thinking of getting married, honey. I wanted to tell you tonight when we were all together. I hope you approve."

"Sure, Daddy," she said. "I want you to be happy. I want to get a picture of the two of you. Daddy, will you bring your chair around beside Megyn?"

Dutifully, Lew did as his daughter told him and Jamie Lynn snapped several pictures with her cell phone camera. "They're beautiful," she said. "You're a beautiful couple. I hope you'll be very happy together. I have to go pee."

Lew chuckled at Jamie Lynn's sudden change of direction. She was a fascinating girl who bewitched everyone who had the good fortune to know her. He couldn't help noticing that, as she hustled off to the ladies' room, every male eye in the restaurant followed her every step. It was something he'd come to accept since she turned sixteen. It made him uncomfortable, but there was little he could do about it.

"She gets a hell of a lot more attention than I do," Megyn said, almost as if she were jealous of the girl.

"Now, Megyn, I was under the impression that my attention was enough for you."

"I'm sorry, Lew," she said. "It is all I need. Jamie Lynn is a beautiful girl. I'm not jealous of her.

I'm going to have the Steak Diane, the eight-ounce, medium," Megyn told the waiter.

Lew ordered the twelve-ounce Pepper Seak, medium rare.

"I'll have what she's having," Jamie Lynn said, pointing at Megyn, "only I want mine medium rare, like my daddy's."

ぐつひつ

"He finally found his Peggy," Abby said when she saw the pictures of Lew and Megyn.

"What do you mean, Mom?" Jamie Lynn asked her.

"This woman looks just like Peggy did, judging from the pictures I've seen of her, I mean."

"Well, I hope he never shows her pictures of his dead wife," Jamie said. "That could ruin his marriage. If this woman comes to believe he married her because she looks just like the wife he lost, it could hurt her very badly."

"You're right, Jamie, but Lew is smart enough to know that. Megyn is beautiful, and apparently very smart, I really hope she makes him happy. I'd hate to see him get hurt again."

"She's not as pretty as you are, Mom," Jamie Lynn said.

"Thank you, darling. You don't have to say that just because I'm your mother."

"I'm not, and she kind of acts like she's smelling fish all the time."

"You mean she's stuck up?" Abby said.

"Yes, but that's not why she's not as pretty as you are, she's just not, really."

"No, she isn't, Abby," Jamie said. "No one is that pretty."

"Thank you, both, my head is big enough."

"Well, put it this way," he added, "You're the prettiest woman I've ever seen."

ぐろゆ

One Saturday morning, Jamie and Abby were still lying in bed. His arm was around her, and her head was resting on his chest while he caressed her shoulder and arm. Jamie Lynn came skipping into the room and hopped up into the bed with them. Squirming her way in between the two of them, she said, "Listen up. Tommy is coming over in just a bit. He wants to talk to Dad."

"What does he want to talk to your dad about, honey?" Abby asked.

"I don't know."

"Oh, I bet you do," Jamie said. "He wants to marry you, and he's going to ask me for my permission."

"That's right," she said. "What are you going to say, Daddy?"

"Well, I don't know. I've only had a daughter for two years now. I'm not sure I can live without you yet. I've grown quite fond of you in the last two years."

"You're teasing me, right, Daddy?"

"Maybe," he said. "What if this boy makes a career of the army and they send him to Mars, or somewhere like that, and he wants to take you with him? What are your mother and I going to do then? I'm serious, now, my darling daughter, I don't want to be a continent, or even a country, away from you, ever. If he ever plans on taking you out of Colorado, then we have a problem. I love you too much too lose you again."

She put her arms around his neck and hugged him tightly. "I promise you, Daddy, I won't ever leave you."

"Thank you, honey," he said. "Listen, Jamie Lynn, ultimately it's your decision who you marry and where you live, but I think you know I am pretty much insane over you and I want you in my life for the *rest* of my life, no matter who you marry. I missed being with you and your mother for fourteen years, and you both are as important as air is to me."

"Air?" she repeated. "You couldn't live a minute without air, Daddy. "You can go a weekend without seeing me without any problem. You do that all the time."

"Yeah, but I don't like it," Jamie said, and Jamie Lynn giggled.

⋐⋑⋐⋑

"I'm not staying in the army, sir. I plan to get a job and stay in The Springs. Jamie Lynn loves it here, and this is where we want to live."

"So do you have any idea what you want to do when you, get out of the service, Tommy?"

"I've thought about it and talked it over with Jamie Lynn and what I'd really like to do is what you do, Mr. Cain."

"You want to work for the park service?"

"Yes, sir, that's what I'd like to do. Do you think I'd be able to maybe get a job doing that?"

"Well, I don't know, but it's something we can look into," Jamie said. "It will help if you have some schooling, but I didn't have much. Let me look into it. I'll help you any way I can. How much time do you have left in the army?"

"About two years, Mr. Cain," Tommy said.

"You're going to have to call me by my first name, Tommy. Mr. Cain is just too formal for me. Just promise me when you and Jamie Lynn have kids you won't name any of them Jamie."

"We won't," he said. "It would sound like an echo chamber in our house."

Tommy's and Jamie Lynn's wedding was scheduled for June of 2005. She was eighteen. The service was to be held at Circle Drive Baptist Church in The Springs. Tommy's mother had been a member of the church ever since she divorced Tommy's father several years earlier. Vera Baker often commented to friends that she had lost Mark Baker and found Jesus, and she got the better part of that deal by far.

Jamie and Abby spent the weekend before the wedding at the cabin in Beulah Valley. Jamie Lynn stayed the weekend with Lew and broached the subject of the wedding and that she wanted her dad, Jamie, to walk her down the aisle.

"I just think he needs to do this, Daddy. I hope you understand. I don't want to hurt either of your feelings." She was very animated as she explained her thoughts on how she arrived at her decision.

"Dad, Lew, that's you," she began. "Well, we've been together all my life, and you know I love you, I always will. Dad, Jamie, is still fascinated and overwhelmed with being a dad. I just can't take any of that away from him at this critical time in his development."

"I do understand, darling, and I'm fine with it. For the man to suddenly find the love of his life after so many years and discover that he has 'you' as a bonus, what a blessing you must be to him. I actually envy him, but I'm happy for him and for you that you have him."

"I'll always have two daddies, Daddy. I'm a lucky girl."

"And those two daddies are lucky men, Jamie Lynn," he said. "Lucky men, indeed."

ℰↄℰↄ

The church auditorium was larger inside than the building looked outside. The seating was divided into several sections that cascaded downward, like a movie theater, toward the choir loft, baptismal tub, and altar.

Tommy's entire Platoon showed up, about fifty men, all in dress greens. They were seated in the center section down front. Twenty men, and four female soldiers, had been chosen to form a cordon out the door of the church as the couple left to go to the reception.

There were fifty or sixty friends of Jamie Lynn from high school and a few from her class at UCCS, who had managed to get out of class. Abby's friend, Lillian Morrow, from work, was sitting with her on the front row.

Lew and Megyn arrived as Jamie and Jamie Lynn were waiting in the corridor of the church. Jamie Lynn ran over to Lew and hugged him then hugged Megyn and then ran back to where Jamie was waiting for the signal to start the walk.

Lew and Megyn went into the auditorium and made their way to a couple of seats in the back. While sitting there waiting for his daughter to be escorted down the aisle to the man she will soon marry, Lew played out the last eighteen years in his mind.

He had graciously accepted Jamie Lynn's reasoning, for wanting her late-to-the-party biological father to walk her down the aisle, without showing her how it had torn him apart. The pain was such that he almost had not recovered from it in time for the wedding. Even now, as he watched her with the man, waiting for the start of the affair that would indelibly scar him forever, his mind conjured up things he could not suppress.

Why did this have to happen? Lew thought. *Why couldn't you just stay—dead—No, I can't have such thoughts. This is not who I am. I'm better than that, I'm a better man than that. But I loved her so much. Abby, God how I loved Abby. My daughter, and she will always be my daughter, she stands there now, like a vision. The gown, picked out by her mother, renders everyone who looks at her breathless. Every man in her presence stares at her, transfixed. She wears a princess crown with the veil hanging in back, nothing covering that beautiful face. The strapless white gown should be saved for posterity after gracing my daughter's flawless personage.*

The music began and Lew came to his senses.

Tommy was in full dress uniform, waiting at the altar with his best man, Jimmy Murdoch.

The organist began playing, and Jamie crooked his left arm for his daughter to take. They began the age-old custom of delivering the man's daughter to the new man in her life. The audience murmured with delight when they saw Jamie Lynn in her wedding dress. There were whispers and audible comments.

"She's so beautiful," one commented.

"Wow, look at her," one boy said.

Jamie looked over at her. *She's Abby, eighteen years ago.*

A million things were going through Jamie's mind as he walked beside this lovely, enchanting creature whom he had been given the good fortune to call his daughter.

He'd never changed her diaper when she was a baby, he'd never sipped tea with her at an imaginary tea party. When she started to school, he had never helped her with her homework. When thunder and lightning had awakened her in the middle of the night, she had never run and jumped into bed with him and her mother. He'd never put a bandage on her knee when she had fallen off her bike. He had missed so much in her life, so much he could never get back. Only one man had been there when she needed him. Only one man had done all those things that Jamie so desperately wished he could have done for her. They had just walked past that man, sitting a few rows back in the pews.

"Hold up a minute, honey," Jamie said to Jamie Lynn. He signaled to the pastor, made the sign for "time out" so he would stop the music, and the organist stopped playing. And, with that, everyone in the room looked at them to see what was going to happen next.

"Wait here just a minute, baby, I'll be right back." Jamie walked back up the aisle to where Lew and Megyn were sitting. The look of astonishment on their faces was almost amusing. Jamie took Lew's hand.

Lew looked at him, still dumbfounded.

"Come on, Lew," Jamie said. "Let's go walk our girl down the aisle."

Lew stood up, tears filled his eyes, and he hugged Jamie. Both men hugged each other, being mindful to administer the obligatory back slapping, in order to send a sufficiently macho signal to all observers that they were indeed of the masculine persuasion. Then they walked back to Jamie Lynn and, one on each side, continued escorting her to the front of the church where her future husband was waiting.

The pastor asked, "Who gives this woman to be married?"

Both Lew and Jamie answered in unison, "We do, we're her fathers."

After the nuptials were complete, Mr. and Mrs. Tommy Baker were escorted out of the church auditorium by Tommy's fellow soldiers. The reception was held in a separate rented hall so the married couple and guests could drink a few beers and dance. Tommy and Jamie Lynn danced, and Jamie and Lew both danced with their daughter.

It was not a wild affair, more a time of reflection for Abby. "I've had her for eighteen years, and now she's gone. What am I going to do, Jamie?"

"Nonsense, honey," Jamie said. "They'll be living less than a mile away. You'll never lose her. She'll always be your daughter."

∽∾∽

When the reception was over, Lew came over and thanked Jamie for what he did. "It meant more than you can ever know, Jamie, thank you."

"It did to me too, Lew, and I know Jamie Lynn will remember it always."

Tommy retrieved his car and pulled around to pick up his bride. They were going to spend their honeymoon at Jamie's cabin. Jamie had stocked it with food and soft drinks, put in a TV with satellite service for them, and promised them they would not be disturbed.

Jamie Lynn waved to her parents out the window of the car as they waved to her from the curb. Then she formed a circle, with the index finger of her left hand, by touching it to her thumb. Then she placed the index finger of her right hand inside the circle and poked in and out in a lewd sexual gesture, all the time beaming from ear to ear.

"Oh my God," Abby said.

Jamie just watched her, wide-eyed. "Did she just do what I think she just did?"

"Yes, she did," Abby replied.

Jamie chuckled. "That boy is going to have an interesting life."

About the Author

Jack Sprouse is from Dallas, Texas, although he now lives in Lewisville, a few miles north of Dallas. He studied American History at Texas Tech, in Lubbock, and his fields of greatest historical interest are the American Civil War and World War II. He served in the United States Navy as a crewmember on an ASW (anti-submarine-warfare) patrol aircraft. Writing fiction is his passion.

Sprouse just loves making stuff up (his mom used to punish him for doing that when he was a kid). He has written two books of historical fiction (*Adventures in Time Book I: The American Civil War* and *Adventures in Time Book II: The American West*—these are both Walter Mitty type stories in which he places himself back in time as a war correspondent following historical events and interviewing the major players in those events; two books of original poetry, *The Quiet Place* and *Dreams of a Forgotten Man*—both books contain approximately fifty original poems on various subjects: life, love, friendship, relationships, war, conflict, tragedy; and several novels: *The House Wren*, a saga of a fictional Texas family; *On Nep-*

tune Wings, a love story set in the 1960s against the backdrop of a US Navy Patrol Squadron; *Magnolia Road*, an improbable love story between a girl from Vermont and a rancher from Colorado. She is purposeful and dedicated to her chosen calling in life; *Clare*, about a twenty-four-year-old woman who faces life with quiet confidence and inner turmoil, experiencing love, hurt, uncertainty, sexual harassment in the workplace, and tragedy; *Magnolia Road*, about a young college student who must chose between true love and her life's calling; and *Dreams Once Dreamed*, about two soul mates who are torn apart by circumstances beyond their control. He is currently working on several ideas for new books.

www.ingramcontent.com/pod-product-compliance
Lightning Source LLC
Chambersburg PA
CBHW051455170626
46811CB00002B/494